Our Last FIRST KISS

Copyright

This is a work of fiction. Names, characters, places, and incidents are either the product of the author's imagination or used fictitiously, and any resemblance to actual persons, living or dead, business establishments, events or locales is entirely coincidental.

All rights reserved.
Our Last First Kiss
Copyright 2018 © Darlene Tallman
Published by: Darlene Tallman
Proofread by: Vera Quinn
Editors: Joanne Dearman, Kat Beecham, Jenni Belanger,
Melanie Gray, Shannon McFadden
Formatting: Liberty Parker
Cover by: Tracie Douglas of Dark Water Covers

ALL RIGHTS RESERVED. This book contains material protected under International and Federal Copyright Laws and Treaties. Any unauthorized reprint or use of this material is prohibited. No part of this book may be reproduced or transmitted in any form or by any means, electronic or mechanical, including photocopying, recording, or by any information storage and retrieval system without express written permission from. Darlene Tallman, the author / publisher.

Author's Note: This book is intended for mature audiences 18+ due to adult content

Table of Contents

Copyright
Table of Contents
Dedication
Acknowledgements
Prologue
Chapter One
Chapter Two
Chapter Three
Chapter Four
Chapter Five
Chapter Six
Chapter Seven
Chapter Eight
Chapter Nine
Chapter Ten
Chapter Eleven
Chapter Twelve
Chapter Thirteen
Chapter Fourteen
Chapter Fifteen
Epilogue One
Epilogue Two
About the Author

Dedication

For those who realized they had to make a change and did whatever they had to in order to make that happen.

One of my former co-workers, Taijuana, was your average-sized mom and several years ago, she decided she was going to run. I have watched her progress with great interest on Facebook. She has completely transformed who she was into a lean, mean, running machine and she competes all over the place. Her children are all athletic as well, and it makes me think of how our children mimic what we do. If we read, they will read. If we enjoy learning, they will apply themselves. If we get out into the world and are active, they will find their passion and play. So in a way, even though this is in no way her story at all, this is dedicated to "T-mama" for her perseverance.

And for you, my reader, I hope you like Thorne and Tinsleigh and their story.

Acknowledgments

I say each and every book that I have the best beta team and I truly believe that with everything in me. These ladies offer opinions on everything from names of characters (sometimes I'll have one but not the other) to which cover would be best (because I have a whole folder of premade covers I've bought and most have no stories). They read the snippets and usually say "more!" And when it comes time, they read the whole manuscript and find those lines that would make great teasers to create, as well as give me input on what needs tightening up. I couldn't do this without them. Jenni has been helping to keep my author page update and also keep me straight during takeovers, and Daverba Ortiz is sharing books far and wide. Plus, I've recently added Nicole Lloyd to my team to promote my work far and wide; she's genuinely a rockstar in the indie community.

I also couldn't do this without my fellow indie authors who I yak with constantly, either on the phone or via messenger or text, who listen as I read a section or help me brainstorm when I'm stuck. The two-way street I've found with #MyTribe of ladies has been beautiful, absolutely beautiful. Some of my closest friends live hundreds and hundreds of miles away these days. Erin, Kayce, and Liberty – the three of you talked me off that proverbial ledge earlier last year, so I have y'all to thank for telling me not to throw in the towel. Cherry? Our time zones notwithstanding, I love seeing your messages pop up, even if it IS an "elebenty nine-one-one"! And I cannot wait until 2018 when we get to meet in Australia!

I also have sweet non-bookworld friends who encourage me on this journey. They'll ask those silly questions like "Have you written today?" or "Which book are you on now?" (the answers are generally 'maybe' and 'all of them' in case you were wondering!).

When I started down this path, my goal was to publish a book and I've done that. Knowing that there are folks who have read several of my books over and over again? Humbling beyond words. I've always said that you never know how your words will impact someone else and some of the messages I've received have been mind-blowing (in a good way). So, as long as folks want to read what I have to say, I'll keep writing.

Prologue

"But...I don't understand," she said, biting her bottom lip to stop the quivering as tears built up a fine mist behind her eyes. She watched, wide-eyed, as her husband, the man she'd been madly in love with since middle school, threw his clothing into a box he'd brought home from work.

"Look, Tinsleigh," he replied as he threw down an armful of clothes, straightening up and turning to face her. He was still as handsome as the day she'd first met him, his dark hair now showing its first silvery strands, his broad shoulders stretching his shirt tight across his chest as he planted his hands on his hips. Hands that used to hold her gently, touch her intimately...

"I don't see how I can be much clearer," he interrupted her reverie, impatience making his voice sharper than usual. "Attraction is what keeps a marriage together, and I'm no longer invested in what you're offering."

"Why are you saying these things?" she gasped, hating herself for letting him see her upset. She was so weak, such a coward. She should have known this was coming. "Are you saying you're not attracted to me anymore?"

"That's exactly what I'm saying," he said, brushing past her and sweeping his toiletries from the bureau into a small bag.

"B-but that doesn't make any sense," she shook her head, her vision blurry as she fought to hold back her tears. She refused to give him the satisfaction of seeing her cry. "I may have gained a couple of pounds over the years, but I'm the same size as I was the day we were married."

"It's *where* those few pounds have settled, my dear," he grimaced, looking pointedly at her hips. "You've let yourself go, Tinsleigh, and I'm sorry, but it's just not there for me anymore." He zipped up his suitcase and hefted it up, carrying it down the hall.

Tinsleigh rubbed her hands over her bare arms as she slowly walked down the hall. Her entire world was crumbling down around her, and she didn't know what to think. As she stepped into the living room, her eyes automatically went to the window, where she could see Denny placing his suitcase into the trunk of his car. Unable to watch a second longer, she spun away from the window, sinking down into the plush settee her parents had gifted them last Christmas. It was her favorite reading chair, but right then it seemed like the perfect place to curl up and die.

Denny walked back into the house, jingling his keys in his hand, as though he hadn't a care in the world. In that moment, Tinsleigh hated him.

He paused when he saw her sitting there, her fingers twisted together in a gnarly, tangled mess. Sighing, he crouched down in front of her, untangling her fingers enough to slip his hands into hers. He said nothing for the longest time, and Tinsleigh couldn't bear to raise her eyes to his, to see the disgust on his face.

Finally, he leaned forward, pressing his lips tenderly against her forehead. "My attorney will be in touch," he whispered, pulling his hands gently away from hers as he stood and backed away.

Tinsleigh squeezed her eyes shut until she heard the front door slam, keeping them closed until she heard the revving of his car engine as he drove away.

When she opened her eyes, she was alone.

At last, the tears began to flow.

Chapter One

One year and ~~fifty~~, no...thirty pounds later

She walked out of the doctor's office, a stack of papers clutched in her hand. As the doctor's words ran through her head, she approached her car and after unlocking it, got in and sat there in disbelief.

"Tinsleigh, I know you've been taking off the weight you gained this past year after your divorce, but your numbers are not good. Right now, you've got several kidney stones which is what is causing the pain you've been having. We'll keep an eye on those, but you may end up having to have surgery if you're unable to pass them. Also, if we don't do something to speed up the weight loss process a bit, you're in real danger of developing diabetes as well."

Once Dr. Day had gone over the numbers with her, she had given her the information for a nutritionist and personal trainer. "He's the best there is, Tinsleigh, and he'll help you achieve the weight loss safely. I also think your thyroid is underactive based on the symptoms you described so I want some blood drawn for that as well. The nurse will be in to get that once we're done."

Thumbing through the papers, she pulled out the pamphlet the doctor had given her for the nutritionist. He had a Master's Degree in Nutrition and was a licensed personal trainer. The picture that stared back at her showed a good-looking man. *Yeah, like someone who looks like that would ever look at me.* Taking a deep breath, she tossed everything into the passenger seat and starting the car, drove home.

He was sitting in his office at the gym when the phone rang. Reaching over, he said, "Hello," unprepared for the gut-punch he got when he heard the female voice on the other end.

"Um, hi. My name is Tinsleigh Aber...I mean, Martin, and my doctor suggested I give you a call."

Grabbing a client intake form, he replied, "Thorne Baker. Can you tell me why your doctor gave you my information?" He was always intrigued whenever someone called and said their doctor wanted them to call.

"Well, over the past year, I gained a lot of weight but then started losing it. Unfortunately, it's not fast enough or something, and she thinks I need a bit of help."

"Do you want to schedule an appointment to come into the gym? I can send you the forms to fill out."

He could hear her deep intake of breath before she replied, "Yes. I think that would be a good idea."

Looking at the calendar, he quickly set up her appointment and then got her email address, so he could send the new client forms to her. "I'll see you Friday, Tinsleigh."

"Thank you, Mr. Baker," she said.

"Thorne. Mr. Baker is my dad."

"Alright, thank you, Thorne. I'll see you on Friday. Do I need to email the completed forms back to you?"

"You can, but we're going over them so it's not necessary."

She nodded even though he couldn't see it, then said, "Okay. I'll let you get back to work then."

Hanging up the phone, she fully exhaled. His voice was what she imagined warm chocolate would sound like, with just a hint of whiskey. Shaking her head at where her mind went, she decided to see if she had any work orders pending.

Standing and stretching, she decided to take a break and meandered into the kitchen to start something for lunch. While it cooked, she threw in a load of laundry and then went through the pile of mail sitting on the kitchen island. *Junk. Junk. Bill. Check.* Opening the check, she smiled. One of her newer clients had paid their outstanding invoices and she did a little jig inside, knowing she would be able to pay off a few things for good and still have money left over to tuck away in savings. When the timer went off, she pulled her meal from the microwave and then sat down at the kitchen table to eat. As she ate, her mind wandered over the past year. Groaning aloud at some of the stupid things she had done post-divorce, she finally pulled the pad of paper she had on the table and grabbed a pen.

Remember, choose to see the positive in things she wrote. *I'm positive this is going to work for me. I'm positive that no matter how hard it gets, I will embrace this diet wholeheartedly.* She continued to write affirmations and goals as she ate. Shortly after Denny left, she found herself adrift, relying on comfort foods to give her solace when her own family turned their backs on her. Within nine months, she had gained almost fifty pounds before reality had intruded. Since then, she had dropped twenty of those pounds, but now she was stuck. *If Denny thought I was unattractive before, he should see me now.*

No, she wasn't going there. He had used that as an excuse to take off with his assistant and as soon as the ink was dry, he married her. Rumor had it that they had a baby boy but she honestly didn't care. *You're still young and you're kind and generous and giving. There's someone out there who will love you, warts and all, whether you lose another pound or not.*

Shaking her head from where her thoughts had drifted, she finished eating then cleaned up the dishes she had used before returning to her office. Opening her QuickBooks program, she recorded the payment that was received, then emailed a current statement to her client reflecting a zero balance. She took a few minutes and got the check ready to deposit, then wrote out the remaining checks for the month. Seeing the ending balance, she grinned and made a note to transfer monies over to her savings account once the deposit was made.

Opening her emails, she saw a new one from a prior client asking if she could take on another job for them. Hitting reply, she quickly typed out a response and attached her new rate sheet. Business had picked up, mostly due to word of mouth, and she was tickled beyond belief at what she had managed to build. Once that was done, she opened the email from Thorne and started filling out the forms he had sent.

Friday morning

Pulling into the gym parking lot, she parked her car and sat there, thinking. Dr. Day had called the day before and told her that she did have an underactive thyroid as well and she would be calling in the prescription. *Here goes nothing.*

As she walked into the gym, she could see people of all sizes working out. *Well, at least I won't stick out too badly.* Smiling at the woman behind the reception desk, she said, "Hi, my name is Tinsleigh Martin and I have an appointment with Thorne this morning."

"He's on a phone call but I'll let him know you're here. Let me show you around while you wait," the young woman said. "By the way, my name is Izzy."

"Hi, Izzy. I'm a little nervous."

"Nothing to be nervous about. Thorne is the best at what he does."

Izzy came from behind the desk and motioned for Tinsleigh to follow her. She stopped at an open office door and said, "Thorne, I'm taking your next appointment to show her around. Come find us when you're done." As she walked by, Tinsleigh caught a glimpse of a dark-haired man with a closely trimmed beard. Izzy took her to the women's locker room, saying, "You'll have your own locker, and we have showers back here as well."

"That's good, although I work from home so it's not as if I can't go home and grab one," Tinsleigh said.

"True, but then again, after one of his workouts, you'll probably change your mind," Izzy replied, laughing. "Let me show you the pool."

They headed through another door and she found herself in the pool area. Each lane was delineated with markers and she watched as several people swam laps. "I enjoy swimming," she murmured. "Used to swim competitively, but that was several years ago."

"It'll come back to you," a deep voice said from behind her.

Turning, she saw the man that had been in the office and had to stop herself from drooling. He was tall. Much taller than her five-foot three-inch frame. Chestnut-brown hair that had a slight wave to it curled along the nape of his neck and his beard, something she never liked before, had her wondering if it would feel soft against her fingers. "Hi, I'm Tinsleigh," she said as she lifted her hand.

"Thorne. I figured I would find you two back here. Izzy? I'll take it from here, okay?"

"You got it, boss-man," the younger woman replied. "Nice to meet you, Tinsleigh. If you have any questions, feel free to ask."

"Thanks, Izzy. Nice to meet you too." *Great, now I'm alone with this hunkalicious man and can't find my words.*

"Come on back to my office and we'll go over your forms," he said.

She said nothing as she followed him out of the pool area and back to his office. A million thoughts ran through her head and she had to mentally shake herself to keep from saying anything.

Once in his office, he motioned for her to sit in the chair in front of his desk and he grabbed a folder. Opening it, he said, "Thanks for emailing the forms back. It makes it easier since I get a chance to look them over beforehand. I've got a few questions I need answered so we can start outlining a viable exercise program for you."

"Okay."

"It says you have run cross country and you also swam competitively. Can you tell me more?"

Taking a deep breath, she said, "I was a state championship runner in high school and ran on the college team as well until I injured myself."

"What kind of injury did you have?" he asked while jotting a few notes.

"I tore my ITB muscle in my hip," she replied.

"Did you have therapy?"

"Once it was healed, yes, but by then, the season was over. When the next year started, the coach didn't want to take a chance that I wasn't fully healed so I didn't make the team."

"That's a shame. Did you keep running?"

"On my own, yes, for a few more years."

"Why did you stop?"

"I got married, started my own business, and got busy setting up a house and it went by the wayside. Since my divorce, I've started jogging again but am nowhere near where I was when I was in college."

"Now tell me about your swimming."

"I was the long-distance swimmer in high school and college. I usually swam the five-hundred yard race."

"How were your times?" he asked, again jotting down a few notes.

"Actually, pretty good. I usually placed in the top three during races and went to state a few times."

He nodded as he wrote. *What is he writing? And why am I so nervous?*

"Okay, one last question. How do you feel about riding a bike?"

"Well, I know how, but I haven't ridden in a long time."

He looked at her and said, "I think I have an idea about your exercise program. Hear me out before you say no off the bat."

"Okay," she said.

"The fact that you've swam and run competitively in the past is something we're going to work with and add in bike riding. I want you to compete in a mini-triathlon. They're called sprint triathlons."

"A triathlon? Me? Have you *looked* at me?" she asked.

"By the time you compete, you'll be in better shape, but folks of all shapes and sizes participate," he advised. "Now, let's talk about what you like to eat."

"I like meat. I like most vegetables and fruits. I won't eat liver or cauliflower, and I prefer raw broccoli."

"So, chicken, steak, pork. What about turkey and fish?"

"Seafood is okay. Nothing with tentacles."

He started laughing at the face she made when she said tentacles. "Okay, so nothing with tentacles and no liver or cauliflower. Got it."

"How hard is this diet going to be?" she asked.

"Tinsleigh, it's not going to be a diet. It's a lifestyle change. No one can 'diet' long-term, but a lifestyle change? It may take some time, but you will see progress, I promise."

She nodded before saying, "Okay, what's next?"

He stood and replied, "Now, we go see what you need to get to be successful."

"What do you mean?"

"We're going to clean out your refrigerator and cupboards of everything that you don't need and then replace it with the things you'll need to properly fuel your body for this journey."

Shit. He was going to see her stash of candy bars. Standing, she asked, "Are you going to follow me?"

"Yes, and then we can take my truck if that's okay. Do you have a bike?"

"No."

"Then we can hit the sports store and get you the equipment you're going to need, okay?" Seeing the look on her face, he leaned closer and said, "It's going to be fine, Tinsleigh. Think of it like this – you're making some major changes and you'll be working hard. I want you to succeed and this is one way I can help ensure you do."

She smiled at his words and he caught his breath. She was gorgeous as she was as far as he was concerned, but when she smiled, she was radiant. *She's the one* resonated deep within his soul.

He followed behind her as she drove to her house, his mind racing. *How is it possible that I've never been attracted to a client before and she walks in and I feel like I'm a teenager again? I've never felt like this before, not even with Marisa.*

Pulling into her driveway, he admired her house. Set back on a few acres, it was a cottage-style house with a stone exterior. Flower beds along the walkway highlighted the whimsical statuary that was interspersed everywhere. A detached, two-car garage had a glass walkway to protect her from the weather getting in and out of her vehicle. He could see large ferns hanging inside the breezeway. Coming up behind her, he took a deep breath. The floral scent she wore was just enough to stir his senses further. Once she got the door unlocked, he followed her inside and stopped. Directly inside the door was a small foyer with a hall closet and an inset shelf where books and knick-knacks resided. To his right was a living room with a comfortable-looking sectional couch and a large television mounted above the fireplace. Straight ahead was a curved archway into the kitchen. Once again, he followed her into the kitchen where she stopped and said, "Okay, where do we start?"

"Do you have any boxes?" he asked. "We can box up anything that's unopened and drop it off at the food pantry."

"I like that idea," she replied. "I've got some out in the garage. I'll be right back."

He looked around the kitchen and noticed the little touches that made it warm and cozy. *Much like her.* When she returned, she had several flattened boxes that she put on the table before going over to a drawer in the kitchen and grabbing some tape and a pair of scissors.

They put the boxes together and he asked, "Do you have a pad of paper and a pen?"

"Why do we need those?"

"We're going to make a list of the things you need to buy."

Shaking her head for not thinking about it, she went to the fridge and grabbed the magnetic pad and the pen and put them on the counter. "Fridge first?" she asked.

"Let's do the cupboards first so the perishables are last in the boxes," he replied.

Walking over to the one set of cupboards, she opened the doors and said, "Here's my pantry."

He stood next to her and softly said, "It's going to be okay, shortstuff." Reaching in, he started taking out the boxes of cereal and looking at the ingredients. "This one is okay but only once or twice a week. Do you eat cereal often?"

"I like it but don't have to have it if it's not necessary."

"No, that's not how this works. If you enjoy cereal, we'll work it into your plan, okay?"

She nodded before asking, "What do I need to look for on the ingredients?"

"Let's try to keep the sugar content down and the protein and fiber content up."

"Okay." She grabbed the next box and looked over the ingredients. "This one should be okay, I think," she said as she handed him the box.

He glanced at it and nodded in agreement. "That one can stay."

They worked their way through her cereal and then he started on her canned goods. "Are you dead-set on canned vegetables?"

"It's more a convenience than anything."

"We'll go over meal preparation too. It will help if one day a week, you make what you're going to eat for the whole week whenever possible. Then, the decision is made and you can just grab a container and go." He went to the pad of paper and she saw him write down *reusable plastic containers.*

By the time they were done with the pantry, she had more empty spaces than full. He then asked what kind of spices she used and she opened the cabinet above the stove. Within minutes, he had removed the majority of them and she said, "How am I going to season anything?"

"You're going to swap the salts for powders. And since I see you have a green thumb, I think you should start an herb garden. Fresh ingredients are better for you because they don't have all the preservatives and additives."

She nodded and went to the pad and wrote *stuff for an herb garden*. "Can we buy fresh stuff at the store since it's going to take some time for a garden to grow?"

"Absolutely."

"I hate you're spending so much time with me to do this," she said.

"You signed on for the works and this is part of it," he replied. *No, it's not, you just want to spend time with her and get to know her.*

"Somehow I doubt that. So, freezer next?" she asked.

"You mentioned you work at home in your forms. Do you have anything in your office?"

She nodded and he watched as her face got red before she mumbled, "My chocolate stash."

Once again, her face had him laughing. "I promise, you can still have chocolate. It's about portion control. Lead the way, Tinsleigh."

He followed her out of the kitchen and down another hallway. Inside her office, she went over to the lower drawer and opened it and started pulling out the various snacks she had stashed away. She wouldn't even look him in the eye as she stacked the bags on her desk. He took the box he had brought in and began putting everything inside. "It's going to be okay, Tinsleigh," he repeated when she still said nothing.

"It's not even like I eat it every day," she said.

"We will get the snack size of your favorites and you can work them into your meal plan," he told her. "Anything else?"

"We still have to get the stuff from out of the freezer, right?"

"Yep. You ready?"

She shrugged. This lifestyle change was a necessity if she wanted to keep on working toward health and according to her doctor, Thorne was the best at what he did. Walking back out into the kitchen, she opened the freezer started pulling things out. "I guess my chicken pot pies are a thing of the past," she said, somewhat mournfully.

He started laughing at the expression on her face. "Not necessarily. Like I said, this is a *lifestyle* change, so if that's something you enjoy, we'll find a way to keep it in your meal plan, okay?"

"Good."

"But these right here," he continued, pointing to the small boxes she had pulled out, "They have to go. Too much junk inside them to even remotely be considered healthy."

"I kind of figured. What about ice cream?"

"Portion control, Tinsleigh. Do I look like I would forego my favorite drinks or meals?"

She looked at him carefully. While he was in phenomenal shape, he didn't strike her as someone who wouldn't occasionally toss back a few beers. "No," she slowly said. "So what you're telling me is that most of what I like I'll still be able to enjoy, just in reduced portions?"

"*Everything* you like, Tinsleigh. If there's a mixed drink you like, you can still have it. Not every night, of course, but if you go out on a girl's night out, you can still enjoy yourself."

"This is good," she mused. "Paige would have a fit if I drank water while she drank margaritas."

He grinned at her as he continued helping her go through the freezer contents. Once everything was out, he jotted more items on the list before saying, "Let's get this packed up and over to the food pantry."

"Okay. Let me grab my debit card since it sounds like we're about to give it a workout."

She walked out of the kitchen to his laughter. *I like his laugh.*

They got everything loaded into the backseat of his truck and then he opened her door for her to get inside. *Damn, it's been a long time since anyone's ridden shotgun with me.* After Marisa, he didn't want anyone riding with him. She had messed with his head and his heart and he had vowed never again. He always met his dates whenever they went out, using work as the excuse. But as he rounded the front of the truck and prepared to get inside, seeing Tinsleigh sitting in the passenger seat gave him a sense of peace he had never had in his life, even with Marisa.

"So what kind of music do you like?" he asked her as he started the truck.

"Pretty much anything, although I'm partial to country," she replied.

He fiddled with the dials until he found the local country station. "Will this work?"

"Yes, thank you. So how long have you been doing this?"

"Played sports throughout high school but saw how inactivity and poor eating choices impacted members of my family. When I lost my grandparents due to complications from diabetes, I changed my major in college. Figured I couldn't save them, but maybe I could give others the tools they needed to be healthier."

"That can't have been easy," she softly said. "Do you have any brothers or sisters?"

"One of each. I'm close with my sister but not my brother."

"I'm sorry you're not close."

"What about you? Parents? Siblings?"

"My folks are still alive, but we don't speak any longer. Well, actually, my mother and I don't speak. I still occasionally see my dad. I've also got two sisters and keep in semi-contact with them."

"Why don't you speak?" he asked. He wanted to know everything about her and decided he wasn't going to question why, he was just going to go with it.

"Me and my mom?"

"Yeah, why don't you speak with her?"

He saw her take a deep breath and was about to tell her not to worry about it when she said, "She's big on the family name and reputation. When my marriage fell apart, she saw it as a black mark against the family name and pretty much disowned me. Dad never stopped her, which has been hard for me, because I always thought we were closer than that, but she rules the roost. I think the thing that bothers me most is it was *him* that ended everything. If my grammy and papaw hadn't left me the house, I would have been up the proverbial creek."

"When did they pass?"

"Oh, years ago, but I stayed there a lot and lived there while I was in college. When they passed, I inherited the house, something my mother wasn't happy about, but Papaw somehow knew that their house was my sanctuary. I rented it out while I was married, but thankfully, it was empty when I needed a place."

"I'm glad you had that in your life. Tell me more about them?" he asked softly.

He watched as her face lit up at the mention of her grandparents. "Grammy was the kind of woman who never met a stranger. She always had room for one more at her table and she's the one who taught me to cook. She would smack me in the head if she saw how I had let things go and was eating all the pre-packaged stuff."

"I think I would have liked your grandma," he said. "There's nothing wrong with occasional easy meals, but when it becomes a way of life, it causes too many problems."

"She taught me how to keep a house, how to sew and quilt, and also how to crochet," she admitted. "Old-fashioned things in this day and age, I know, but I've always enjoyed being able to create something with my hands, you know?"

"Do you make time to do that now?"

"Not as much as I used to, but a lot has happened this past year, and I've been slowly getting back to it. In fact, I'm working on a few things to enter into the local fair."

"Then we'll need to make plans to go when they've been entered to see how you did," he told her. "Okay, give me a few and I'll drop this stuff off."

"I can help."

"I know you can, but it'll only take a few minutes."

She waited in the truck while he carried everything into the food pantry. *Tinsleigh, you know he'd never be interested in the likes of you. He's just your personal trainer. He wants to help people get healthy. That's all this is and nothing more.* And yet somehow, she didn't believe what she was thinking. There was *something* there, but she was a little too gun-shy to pursue it. If he was interested, he was going to have to make the moves.

Chapter Two

He pulled up to the sporting goods store and motioned for her to wait. As he rounded the front of the truck, she admired how he looked and then shook her head. *Not going there, Tins. Nope.* She smiled at him when he opened the passenger door. Helping her down, she felt the shock of his touch down to her toes. *Fuck my life. Why now, God?* Locking the truck, he walked alongside her as they headed into the store, where he grabbed two carts. "Why two carts?" she asked, taking the one he pushed in her direction.

"Well, you're going to need a few things, plus a mountain bike and that gear. Figured the smaller stuff could go in yours and I'll haul the bike," he replied as he navigated over to the shoe section. Spotting a salesman, he said, "She needs workout shoes, running shoes for a triathlon, and biking shoes."

The salesman smiled, saying, "Sounds like a plan. Let's get your feet measured."

She sat down on the bench he indicated and slipped off her shoes. Once he got her measurements, he brought over several boxes of each type of shoe for her to try on. Looking up at Thorne, she started giggling.

"What's so funny?" he asked as he watched her slip on the first pair.

"I don't think I've ever gone shoe shopping with a man before."

He crouched down in front of her after she had the shoes on and checked where her toes were and how the support felt. "Stand up, Tinsleigh, and walk for me," he said. Standing, she walked away for a few steps and then turned and came back towards him. "How do they feel?"

She wiggled her toes experimentally and bounced a little. "Pretty good, actually."

"Okay, we'll take these," he told the salesman. "Now for the running shoes, shortstuff."

Taking off the first pair, she put the running shoes on and he could see from her expression they weren't as comfortable. Again crouching in front of her, he slipped them off and turned to the salesman. "I think she needs a half size bigger on this pair." Looking back at her, he said, "Different manufacturers have slight variances sometimes. That's why I wanted you to try each pair on since it'll be important that you don't rub your feet raw when running."

"Makes sense to me." She waited while the salesman went and got the next size up and when he returned, she put them on. "These feel much better. I thought my toes were going to be squished in the other pair," she told the two men.

"Let's get two pair of these since you'll need a practice pair and a race pair. We'll be sure to break the race pair in, of course, but you'll need the better grip on a newer pair for races."

"You're the boss," she replied.

Damn, I like her spunk. "Okay, now the biking shoes, please," he said to the salesman. The man hurried off and came back with two different styles. After trying them on, he asked, "How do they feel?"

"My toes have enough room and I don't feel like I'm slipping and sliding in them."

"That's good. We don't want blisters during the bike phase since it will make your run a lot harder." Nodding to the salesman, he said, "We'll take these. Do you get paid commission?"

"We get paid hourly plus a commission," the salesman said.

"Then stick with us because I think we're about to make your day," Tinsley quipped. "What's next, boss-man?"

He grinned at her, enjoying her spunky personality. "We want to see the fitness watches. You know the ones that help count calories and such?"

The salesman nodded and said, "Follow me."

"What's your name?" Tinsleigh asked him as she followed behind after putting the boxes with her new shoes in her cart.

"Pete."

"Well, Pete, help me work my debit card out, would ya?" she said, laughing.

He grinned back at the petite woman before glancing up at the man who was beside her. "I appreciate it more than you will ever know."

They made their way to the watches and she watched Thorne look each of them over before finally settling on one. "This one right here will give you a lot of information, shortstuff."

"Besides the time of day?"

"Including the time of day."

"Like what?" she asked.

"Calories burned, heart rate, intensity. And since you'll be swimming, we need one that is waterproof."

"Let me see," she said, taking the small watch-like band from him. He showed her how to turn it on and she clicked through to see the different things he had mentioned. "Will this help you keep track as well?" she asked.

"I'll be taking measurements once a month, but this will help us both know when you reach your target heart rate."

"Okay then let's get this one," she replied as she took it off and put it back in the box before setting it in the cart. "What's next?"

"Running gear, biking gear, and swimming gear," he told her. "And a mountain bike and the accessories."

"What kind of accessories?"

"A helmet, maybe some pads initially when we go out on the trails, and the water bottle attachments."

"How does all that work, Thorne?" she asked.

"By the time you finally compete, you'll know the process inside and out, I promise. But, the short answer is, when you arrive on race day, you get everything set up in the transition area. That includes water bottles and snacks on your bike so that you can refuel a bit before you run."

She nodded even though what he said sounded like Greek. "Okay. Going to trust you on that one because right now, you're speaking a foreign language."

At her comment, he burst out laughing. "I think you're going to be just fine, shortstuff."

Pete, listening to the two of them, asked, "Which did you two want to look at first?"

"Let's look at the swim gear first," Thorne suggested.

Leading the way once again, Pete took them to another part of the store. "Did you want racing suits or what?" he asked.

Thorne thought for a moment. "The race I'm thinking of, she'll wear a racing suit then transition into a pair of biking shorts over her suit. She's going to need something that is snug enough to prevent drag but not so snug that she risks chafing."

Chafing? What the ever-loving-fuck was he getting her into? Looking at him she merely asked, "Chafing?"

"Yeah, Tinsleigh. In the Olympics, the athletes pretty much wear their swimsuit through the whole race, but we're not going for the Olympics, so you can afford to be a bit more comfortable. If we get you a pair of shorts that will work to wick away the excess water from the swimsuit that you can wear to bike and also run in, even better. Pete, do you have anything like that?"

Pete, going through the suits, stopped and looked at the couple he was assisting. "I think we've got something that will work, yes. Do you know the size of your swimsuit?" he asked Tinsleigh.

She blushed. Then she stammered. Finally, she sighed. "Well, hopefully by the time I'm doing this thing, it will be smaller," she replied. "How do the sizes go? Large? Medium? That kind of thing? Or are they in actual size range, like sixteen/eighteen?"

"We have them both ways. Why don't you look through these and pick a few out to see which will be most comfortable?" he asked the young woman. He had seen her blushing and figured that she was probably embarrassed to tell them what size she wore. He didn't see anything wrong with her. She had a lush, curvy figure and if the man standing near her watching her like a hawk wasn't there, he would have asked her out.

She grabbed a couple of suits and said, "I'll go try these on." Headed toward the fitting room, she missed the gleam in Thorne's eyes. After trying both suits on, she decided on the one that was higher cut up the thighs. As she headed back out to Pete and Thorne, she grimaced and then realized this was just another step in reclaiming her health. "I liked this one best," she said as she hung the one she didn't choose back on the rack. "What's next?"

"Swim goggles and a cap," Thorne said as he headed further down the aisle. Once she had picked those out, she looked at him expectantly.

"Let's look at shorts," he told Pete.

Pete led them to another aisle then stepped aside as Thorne went through the rack to find what he had in mind. "Tinsleigh? This is what I was thinking of for you," he told her as she came alongside him. *Damn, she doesn't even come to my shoulder!*

Smiling at him, she searched for her size and then pulled out several pair. "I know I'll be getting smaller ones at some point, but if I have to bike and run now, I'll need more than one pair so I'm not washing clothes all the time."

"Makes sense to me," Thorne replied.

Pete, looking at the cart again, spoke up and asked, "Bikes next?"

"Yes," Thorne stated.

He led them back to the furthest corner of the store where racks of bikes were displayed. "How tall are you?" he asked Tinsleigh.

"Hmm, I think five feet three inches? Something like that, anyway."

Going over to the racks, he found the size she would need and pulled it down. "See how this one feels."

She got on the bike and saw she was able to stand comfortably. "Thorne? What do you think?"

"Let me hold it steady and you see how it feels when you're sitting and stretching toward the handlebars," he replied. "Pete, can you give me a hand?"

She waited for the two men to stabilize the bike before she 'assumed the racing position' and found she was comfortable.

Getting off the seat, she once again stood with both feet on the ground and grinned at Thorne. "I like this one!"

"You look good on it, shortstuff," he replied, grinning back at her. "Pete, I think we're done here, lead the way to the checkout register!"

Everything loaded back in his truck, he helped her in once again and then said, "Let's hit the grocery store now while we're on a roll."

"Sounds like a good idea to me."

As he drove to the local grocery store, he wondered how she felt about all the changes. "Tinsleigh?"

"Hmm?"

"I know this is a lot to get used to, are you okay?"

"I think so, yes. I mean, I've got a lot to process, but I'm sure you're not getting me into a race tomorrow, so I should be okay."

He started laughing at her comment. "No, we're not jumping into any races just yet."

"Good to know," she replied, giggling. "Do I need to add anything to my list?" she asked.

"I don't think so, but we're going to be in there for a bit, so I'm sure there will be additions," he replied as he pulled into the parking lot and found a space. "I know it's all overwhelming, but we're going to take it one step at a time, okay?"

She waited for him to come around and open her door since she needed help getting down. "Thank you," she said once her feet were back on the ground. "Let's go see how much damage we can do in here!"

He chuckled as he led her into the store, grabbing two carts. "We may need more than this, but it's a good start," he told her. "Now, the best way to help yourself when you're undergoing such a dramatic lifestyle change is to shop around the store."

"What do you mean?" she asked.

"If you think of the store as a huge circle, you shop around the edges where all the fresh stuff is, like the produce, meats, seafood. Most of the processed goods are on the aisles."

"That makes sense, I guess," she replied. "Lead the way, boss-man!"

He walked over to the produce section and they spent about thirty minutes getting the vegetables and fruits she liked. While walking, he told her that he would have a better meal plan worked up by the next day, but he would give her an easy one for the next day before she came to work out.

"I'm working out today," she told him with a grin.

"Hmmm, not really."

"Yeah, really."

"How so?"

"My debit card is getting a work out," she replied, laughing at the look that crossed his face.

"That it is, shortstuff. That it is," he responded, his chuckle evident in his tone of voice.

By the time they were done, they had three full carts and her head was swimming with information. He had found the containers she would need for her weekly meal prep, so she got those, as well as the starter plants for her herb garden. As she looked at the carts with the extra items, she started laughing again. "What's so funny?" he asked.

"Where are we fitting all of this?"

"It'll fit, shortstuff."

"Are you sure?" she asked, as the cashier began ringing them up.

"Positive. Have faith."

Well, it's a good thing that check came when it did she thought as the total flashed on the display. While the clerk and bagger put her purchases in the cart, she slid her debit card through the card reader. "Do you need help out?" the teenaged boy asked once they had all the groceries bagged and in the carts.

"Please," she replied. Then, turning to the cashier, she said, "I wish you made a commission on your sales because this would have been a good one!"

The cashier started laughing and said, "Thank you for making my day today."

"I'll definitely be back, although I don't think future purchases will be this large," Tinsleigh told her as she took the receipt. "Thanks again. Have a great day."

When they made it to the truck, Thorne got it started and then made her get in, saying, "This young man and I will get it loaded."

Realizing she wouldn't win the argument, she got in and saw she had a missed text from her best friend, Paige.

Paige: Hey girl, what are you doing?
Tinsleigh: Just finished at the grocery store, why?

Paige: I went and joined that gym you're going to

Tinsleigh: Why?

Paige: Because I'm going to be your support system and that means working out with you.

Tinsleigh: Are you kidding?

Paige: Nope.

Tinsleigh: Don't make me cry with a hottie right outside!

Paige: Whatever. What time do you have to be there tomorrow to work out?

Tinsleigh: I don't know, I'll ask Thorne and hit you back.

Paige: Okay. Later!

He got into the truck after tipping the bagboy. "Thorne?" she asked once he was settled in and buckled.

"What?"

"What time do I need to be there in the morning to work out?"

"Can you work out from nine until eleven every day? We'll do different things and I'll work in rest days for you, but I need to know if you can commit two hours at every workout."

She thought about her workload and realized that she could do the majority of it any time. Looking at him, she said, "Yes, it shouldn't be a problem."

Grabbing her phone and opening up her text messages again, she sent one to Paige.

Tinsleigh: Nine. Will work out for two hours on the days he says.
Paige: Nine it is, I'll see you then.

Glancing over at him as she put her phone up, she said, "Sorry about that. Seems my best friend plans to be my support system in this and she joined the gym and plans to work out alongside me."

"I don't have a problem with that if it helps keep you motivated," he told her as they headed back to her house.

"Good, because we've been through everything together. She doesn't really need to lose any weight, though, so I hope she compensates for whatever she burns off."

"I'll mention it to her tomorrow, okay?" he replied.

Back at her house, they carried in bag after bag until her kitchen had bags on every available inch of counter space. Taking the plastic containers, she got them into the sink in some warm soapy water so she would be ready for her food prep. As they put stuff away, she wondered why he was still there. It seemed he was going above and beyond, and she didn't understand.

"Thorne? I appreciate the help but don't understand why you're still here."

He grabbed the package of salmon they had picked up and after washing his hands, turned on the oven to preheat it before taking some of the fresh herbs and a lemon and bringing them over to the island. "Can you grab a baking pan?" he asked her as he opened the salmon. Once she handed him the baking pan, he sprayed it down with some coconut oil and then seasoned the salmon with the herbs and lemon. "I didn't think you would want to cook tonight after all of this shopping. This is one of the quickest and easiest recipes I know, and I thought I would share it with you. Is that okay?"

Hmm, a meal with a hunkalicious man? Hell yes! "It's fine. I just don't want you to put yourself out for me and I definitely don't want to make your girlfriend angry."

Girlfriend? He didn't have those – he had friends with benefits, not that he was going to tell her that fact. "No steady girlfriend and even if I had one, this is sometimes needed with this job and she would have to understand that fact." *Liar, liar, pants on fire.*

Yay! No girlfriend! As her inner cheerleader geared up to celebrate, she quickly squashed those thoughts. *You're not his type, goofy. He's doing this because it's his job.*

He watched the myriad of emotions as they crossed her face and deduced that she didn't think he would be interested in her. Deciding now wasn't the time to change her mind, he put the pan of salmon in the oven and set the timer. "Do you want to make the salad?" he asked.

Anything to keep my hands busy. Moving to the refrigerator, she grabbed the items she needed and placed them on the island. Getting a colander, she soaked the lettuce before chopping the tomatoes and peeling and quartering the cucumbers. Giving the salad a critical eye, she went back to the fridge and pulled out a yellow bell pepper and quickly cleaned it before dicing it up and putting it in the bowl. "We forgot to get dressing!" she exclaimed.

"No we didn't. Let me show you a different way to flavor your salads," he told her, going over to the spice cabinet and picking out a few of the bottles. He then got the olive oil she had bought and, in a bowl, mixed that and some of the herbs before he drizzled it over the salad. "Where are your tongs?" he asked.

She went to the drawer by the stove and pulled out the tongs and handed them to him and watched as he tossed the salad to spread the dressing. He then got the asparagus out and cleaned it before he prepared it with a little bit of lemon and some pepper. "Can you get me a microwaveable plate?" he asked once he had the asparagus ready. She went to the cabinet and pulled out a plate. He took the plate and got the asparagus going.

Getting plates and silverware, she set the table and asked, "What do you want to drink?"

"Water's fine, shortstuff," he replied.

He got the salmon out of the oven and brought it to the table while she got the asparagus and salad. Once their plates were made, they sat and ate.

Chapter Three

Ugh. Why on earth did I say I would start today? Stumbling out of the bed after a late night spent editing and then researching triathlons, she made her way to the bathroom where she took care of business and then got in the shower to get ready. Thorne had written down her food menu for today, promising to have a more detailed plan when she got to the gym. She quickly dressed then pulled her hair up in a ponytail before heading into the kitchen to make a light breakfast.

While she ate, she jotted down what she would need to buy so she could make sure she was prepared for her food prep. *I'll probably add to this list once I have the food plan.* Oh well, Paige was always good for a shopping trip so hopefully she would come along. Glancing at the clock, she cleaned up the kitchen then went and grabbed her new workout bag, making sure she had a clean outfit as well as her beauty products, so she could get ready at the gym.

Pulling up to the gym, she saw she was fifteen minutes early. *Here goes nothing.* Walking in, she saw that the same woman was behind the desk. "Good morning, Izzy," she called out.

"Good morning, Tinsleigh. You ready for this?"

"As ready as I'll ever be, I guess," she replied as she signed in. "My friend, Paige, is meeting me here."

"Ah, yeah, she came and joined yesterday. Said something about having your back," Izzy remarked.

"And I do," Paige called out, coming up next to Tinsleigh. "Do we have lockers?"

"You do," Izzy replied. "Follow me so we can get your stuff squared away. Thorne is a stickler for starting on time."

Izzy took them to the locker room and gave them their combinations, telling them to head to the gym room. Once she left, Tinsleigh looked at her friend and said,

"Thank you. You didn't have to do this, you know."

"You kidding me? We've been best friends for how many years? When haven't we supported one another, Tiny?"

Tinsleigh laughed at the nickname. Paige's little sister was several years younger than them and wasn't able to say Tinsleigh when she was little, so she had called her Tiny and the name had stuck. "Let's get this party started," she said after locking up her bag and purse.

Walking into the gym, she saw Thorne standing and self-consciously smoothed her shirt down. "Holy smokes, he's hot," Paige whispered as they crossed the gym floor.

"Good morning, Tinsleigh. You must be Paige?" he asked the two women as they stood in front of him.

"I am, yes."

"Okay, let's get the nuts and bolts out of the way. Did you eat the breakfast I outlined?"

She glanced up at him and nodded. "It seemed like a lot of food, but I did eat it all."

"You'll use it, trust me. Now, let me get your measurements and stuff so we have a starting point."

"I don't want to know where I'm at," she quickly said.

"Then I won't tell you," he replied. "I usually do this once a month, so you can see if progress is being made, but if you don't want to know, I'll simply tell you that you're on the right track. How's that?"

"That's fine. I guess what I'm saying is I know I could get hung up on the numbers and miss the fact that my clothes fit better or things are improving medically."

He smiled as he jotted down numbers, quickly getting her measurements while she continued to talk. "You're right. It's *not* all about the number on the scale. How a person's overall health is, how they feel about themselves – those are just as important. And besides, you don't really have much to lose in the grand scheme of things."

Within minutes, he had all her physical stats notated and was walking them over to the board he had hanging on one wall. "Here's where your workouts will be listed. Anything you don't know how to do, I will show you before you get started. When it comes to biking days, we will take your bike out on some trails that are nearby. You'll know ahead of time, so don't worry, okay?"

She looked at the board and saw her name and what her workout was for the day. "So, that's it? I come in and look at the board and then get started?"

"Yes, unless it's a new exercise. Then I'll show you how to do it correctly. And sometimes, I'll be out here to keep you motivated."

"That's what I'm here for, chief," Paige said.

"Today, though, I'll be out here the whole time," he said. *Who am I kidding? I'll be out here every time she comes in.*

Two hours later, sweaty and exhausted, she looked at him and said, "Are you trying to kill me?"

He burst into laughter at the look on her face before sobering and said, "No, shortstuff. You did well for your first day."

"I have sweat in places that shouldn't have sweat!" she exclaimed as she pushed loose tendrils behind her ears. "But I have to admit, it feels good to use my muscles like this again. It's been too long."

"You'll definitely feel it as the day goes on, so I want you to prepare to do some pool work on Monday. I remember you said you had started jogging again so maybe a light jog tomorrow and some stretches since the gym isn't open. You both did well, just remember to keep hydrating today. And you might want to soak in some Epsom salts tonight before bed."

"I feel like a little old lady right now," she murmured to Paige as he walked away.

"Girl, that man is F-I-N-E,"

"He won't be interested in the likes of me, Paige. I'm not his type."

"You don't know that, Tiny. Stop bashing yourself like that."

She rolled her eyes at her friend as they entered the locker room. Quickly unlocking her locker, she grabbed her shower gear and headed into one of the shower stalls. She knew what she was and what she wasn't and regardless of how gorgeous and nice Thorne Baker appeared to be, he wasn't the one for her.

Chapter Four

Three weeks later

Pulling up to the gym, she got out and unlocked her bike from the rack she had installed. Thorne had texted her to say that they would be taking the bikes out today since it was so nice. *I like him. He's attentive without being creepy about it and has been helpful each time we've come.* Paige had begged off today and she was a little nervous about what they would talk about but figured she would take her cues from him.

She walked through the front door and got signed in and then went over to the board. As she was looking at what was coming up over the next week, he came out of his office and strode toward her. *Paige was right, he's mighty fine.* "Good morning, Thorne," she said as he stopped next to her.

"Morning, shortstuff. I figured we would stretch first before we headed out."

"Sounds like a plan to me. I made sure to bring a few full water bottles since I didn't know how far we were biking today," she replied as she got down on the mat and began to stretch.

Damn, she was hot before but now, working out and training like she was, her lush curves were getting toned. Down boy he told himself as he joined her and started stretching. "Not too sure. There are trails nearby that we'll ride today, and we have the ability to stop and start as needed. I figured a leisurely ride would be good since most of what you'll be doing requires stamina. The speed will come."

"You're the boss," she said, continuing her stretches. When she was done she glanced up and saw him standing there, his hand outstretched to help her up. Placing her hand in his, she allowed him to pull her up, doing her best to ignore the tingles that shot up her hand at his touch.

"C'mon, Tinsleigh, the day's wasting away. Did you bring sunblock? If not, I've got some."

"I put some on already and have a bottle in my bag if we're out long enough that I need to apply more."

He placed his hand at the small of her back to lead her out of the gym and to their bikes. Grabbing hers, he mounted it to his truck and then helped her inside.

"How have you been feeling?" he asked once they were both buckled up and he had pulled out into traffic.

"Pretty good. That first week was rough, I'm not going to lie, but I uncovered my treadmill and walked at night to help."

"What do you mean 'uncovered your treadmill'?" he asked.

She blushed before saying, "Um, it was being used as an extra closet."

Bursting into laughter, he replied, "I see. So now you have to use your real closet?"

"Ha ha, very funny!"

"How did I miss this when we cleaned out your cabinets?" he mused.

"Maybe because I don't have any junk food in my room?"

"That could be the reason. Unless you *do* have junk food in your room?"

"Nope. I cleaned that out on my own when I started this process," she told him.

"And the eating plan is working so far?"

"Yeah. I've been experimenting with some different recipes which is fun."

He pulled into the trail parking lot and parked the truck. Helping her out, he got their bikes down and asked, "Do you need help with your helmet?"

"I don't think so. Too bad we can't wear pads during the triathlon," she replied as she got her helmet situated and buckled, then slid on knee and elbow pads. Taking her water bottles, she attached them to the frame and looked at him before saying, "I think I'm ready."

As they rode they talked. She told him about one of her repeat customers who got behind and then expected her to burn the midnight oil. "What did you end up doing?"

"I emailed her back and told her that our contract gives me two weeks to review and edit and she was only giving me one and that wasn't acceptable. She emailed back and offered more money."

"Did you do it?"

"Of course! I mean, healthier food is pricier, don't you know?" she asked, laughing. "It wasn't a lot more, but I let her know that it meant I had to shift other things around and that wasn't fair to anyone else I am working on right now."

"How does that impact your time?" he asked, genuinely curious. She was at the gym six days a week for two hours at a stretch, not counting her commute.

"I got up a little earlier and stayed up a little later," she admitted.

"You know rest is as important as everything else you're doing."

"I know, believe me. I didn't do anything last Sunday except make my meals and work on my entries for the fair since they're due tomorrow."

They had been riding for a while when they came across a break in the trail that led to a small diner. "Do you want to get something to eat?" he asked.

"Sounds good to me. Nice of them to put that here, don't you think?"

He led her to the diner and they locked their bikes on the rack before heading inside. "It was a good business decision for the owner, that's for sure. This trail goes on for quite a few miles and there are other cutaways like this for folks to stop and take a break. We'll eat and turn around to go back."

She smiled at him and his breath caught in his throat. *You're going to have to tell her that you're interested in her as more than a client.* He was about to say something when he heard another female say, "Thorne? What are you doing here?"

Glancing over, he saw his latest 'friend with benefits' Carmen and he internally groaned. "Hello, Carmen. We're out riding today. This is…" he started to say.

"Tinsleigh, how have you been?" Carmen asked, looking the other woman up and down with a slight sneer on her face. "You look…nice."

Tinsleigh pasted a smile on her face and said, "I'm good, Carmen. How have you been?" *Like I give a shit, you mean girl!*

"So, you're working out with Thorne, huh? They say he's the best and if anyone can help you, he can."

What a bitch! "Yes, he definitely knows his stuff."

Thorne, watching the interaction between the two women, saw how Tinsleigh was shrinking into herself at the other woman's words. Realizing that they had a history and it wasn't pleasant, he pulled Tinsleigh close before saying, "It was good seeing you,

Carmen. We need to eat so we can head back."

Deciding to get one last dig in, Carmen said, "I'm sure I'll be seeing you soon, Thorne. Good luck, Tinsleigh!"

Once they had placed their orders, he asked, "How do you know Carmen?"

She grimaced before replying, "We went to school together."

"I gathered the history wasn't all that good."

"You would be correct. She made mine and Paige's lives hell in high school. Seems that she hasn't changed a lot, which is a shame."

"What do you mean?"

"Ah, nothing. Just me, I guess."

"No, I saw how her comments affected you. Can you tell me why?" he softly asked.

She huffed out a breath before saying, "She was the cheerleader and I was the athlete. I was the nerd and she was the party girl. I get along with almost everyone and she looked down on anyone who wasn't in her circle. We clashed a lot because her flavors of the week were always friends with me, and she couldn't understand how that could be possible. More than once she accused me of trying to steal a guy away from her, as if that would even be on the table."

"Why wouldn't it be? You're a beautiful woman, Tinsleigh."

"Um, thank you. But I'm not in her league. Never have been and honestly? I don't ever want to be if it means I have to treat others the way she does."

He sat back and thought about Carmen. Generally, they met for a quick dinner then he would go to her house for a few hours. The few times he had met her elsewhere with a group of friends, he noticed she would be almost sickly sweet with her comments to others around her. *Why did I not notice she was a grade A bitch before?* "I think you're in a league all your own," he finally said.

"Make sure you stretch when you get home," he told her as he mounted her bike back on her car. "I enjoyed today a lot, shortstuff. We need to do it again sometime."

"I'd like that, Thorne. I had a good time as well."

"See you Monday, then?"

"I'll be here."

Chapter Five

He tossed the mail on the side table before heading to the kitchen for a beer. Taking a long pull, he headed in to take shower, his mind on the woman he had spent the afternoon with. As the hot water pounded down on his shoulders, his thoughts turned to the lush curves that had captivated him from the moment she walked into the gym. A low groan erupted as his body reacted to images of her working out, stretching, swimming in that delectable one-piece suit. Reaching down, he gripped himself, slowly stroking and pulling as he replayed every detail of the hours they had been together. Her laugh. Her sass. Her feistiness whenever he pushed her to do more. The way her hair trailed down her back. How her yoga pants covered her luscious hips and ass. Stroking harder now, he imagined her lips around him, taking him to the base as she fondled his balls. Now leaning against the back of the shower, panting as though he had run a marathon, he increased his movements until he felt the familiar tingling shoot up his spine. With a shout, he called out her name as his come shot against the opposite wall. Breathing heavily, he groaned at where his thoughts had taken him, then he realized that he hadn't come that hard in a long time, even when he was regularly seeing Carmen. *Time to tell Tinsleigh how you feel, old man.*

Sitting on his deck, mail in hand, he saw the cream-colored envelope and mentally groaned. His sister, Gloria, had said she was sending her wedding invitation and it looked like it had arrived. *"Thorne, please, you have to come!"* she had exclaimed. *"I know you and Roger have issues now thanks to that skank, but I need my big brother."* He had agreed to go, knowing he would come face-to-face with *them*, but damn, he really didn't want to go. Opening the envelope, he saw the handwritten note at the bottom and smiled. She had put hearts and flowers and underlined the word 'please' multiple times. Picking up the phone, he dialed her number then held the phone away from his ear at her squeal.

"Thorne! Did you get it?" she asked.

"Just got here today, G," he replied. "You know if I didn't love you, I wouldn't be there, right? No desire to see either Roger or her whatsoever. Wait, can you *not* invite them?" he asked his sister.

"I know you don't want to see them. I think they're staying at Mom and Dave's house, so you should be okay to stay at Dad and Sienna's if you want. That's where I'll be."

"Then I'll give Dad a call and make sure it's okay. Are you getting excited?"

"What do you think? I've been planning my wedding day since I was a little girl!" she said, laughing. "How are you doing, Thorne?"

"I'm good. In a good place, business has picked up and I'm…content."

"No one special?"

He thought about Tinsleigh and how much time they'd spent together since she had started working out. "Maybe."

"Maybe? What does that mean?"

"It means, Nosy Rosy, that I have met someone, but I've been taking it slow. She can't see how extraordinary she is yet."

"Will you tell me about her at least? How did you meet? What is she like? Would I like her?"

He started laughing. Leave it to Gloria to get to the heart of the matter. "Her name is Tinsleigh and I met her when she came looking for a personal trainer. She's about your height and yes, I think you would like her a lot."

"More than Carmen?" she inquired.

Grimacing, he nodded, then realized she couldn't see and said, "Probably. Why didn't you like Carmen?" Months ago, Gloria had come for a visit and he had taken her out, running into Carmen who had insinuated that they were more than just *friendly* and ever since, his sister had been trying to fix him up with someone else, claiming that he deserved better than a snake in the grass.

"Are you kidding? That woman makes *her* look like a choir member! She's not a nice person, Thorne and she was nasty to me when you weren't around."

Now he *knew* he was done with Carmen. First, he didn't like how she had treated

Tinsleigh today, but then to find out that she had been nasty to his sister, that definitely put her in the rearview mirror. Besides, all of his thoughts were consumed by a petite female who had no idea just how much she was coming to mean to him.

"I'm sorry, G, that she was nasty. Trust me, she's no longer in any picture."

"So, are you coming then? Can you bring Tinsleigh?"

"You know I wouldn't miss your wedding, even if they'll be there. And, I don't know if Tinsleigh can come or not, but I'll ask her, how's that?" he asked.

"I can't wait to meet her," Gloria enthused.

"She hasn't said yes, silly."

"She will once you turn on your charm, Thorne! Okay, I love you and all that jazz, but I have to run. Me and the girls are going out."

"Be careful. See you in a few weeks. Try not to run Travis ragged, okay?"

"I will. Talk soon. Bye!"

He hung up the phone and sipped his beer as he thought. Before he could change his mind, he opened up his texts and sent one to Tinsleigh.

She had just finished watering her herb garden when she heard her phone chime with an incoming text. Picking it up, she gasped in surprise seeing it was from Thorne.

Thorne: Hey Tinsleigh
Tinsleigh: Hey Thorne, what's up?
Thorne: Didn't you say you were dropping your things off at the fair tomorrow?
Tinsleigh: Yes
Thorne: Mind if I tag along?

At his response, her heart started pounding. She had been attracted to him from the first time she heard his voice, but her experience with Denny had left her doubting her ability to attract anyone.

Thorne: You still there?
Tinsleigh: Yes. Are you sure?
Thorne: Absolutely. What time were you planning to go?
Tinsleigh: I thought I'd head out around ten

Thorne: How about I pick you up around nine and we go get breakfast?
Tinsleigh: That sounds good
Thorne: I'll see you then. Good night, shortstuff
Tinsleigh: Night Thorne

He smiled as he set his phone down. Operation Tinsleigh was now fully in effect.

She got up early the next morning and ran on the treadmill to clear her head. Last night after his text, she had called Paige and gotten some much-needed best friend words of wisdom. While she still wasn't completely sure that he was interested in her, she was trusting Paige who had said 'girl, you don't see how that man watches you when you're not looking!'

Workout now done, she headed into the bathroom to grab a shower. Paige had also said she should ask him, but she didn't have the guts for that at all. Nope. Not a chance in hell she would ask him if he was interested in her. Once done, she got dressed and smiled at how much better she looked already in her leggings. She had always been curvy even in high school and college and was happy to see that she was toning her curves. She had just grabbed the boxes with her fair entries when she heard the doorbell ring. Putting them on the side table by the door, she opened it to a smiling Thorne. "Good morning, Tinsleigh," he said as he stepped inside.

"Morning, Thorne. Is it cold out?" she asked.

"Just a little chilly. A perfect fall day, quite honestly. Can I carry anything out?"

"I have these boxes, but I need to grab my purse and a jacket."

He waited by the door for her to come back with her jacket slung over one arm and her purse over her shoulder before he picked up the boxes she had on the side table. "You ready?" he asked.

"I am, yes."

He put the two boxes in the backseat before opening the passenger door for her and helping her inside. She started laughing once he was inside the truck. "What's so funny?"

"You realize that pretty much every time we are together, we're getting something to eat, right?" she replied, still giggling.

"Well, we *do* need to fuel our bodies since we work out," he retorted.

"True. Just caught me as funny, is all."

He reached his hand over and placed it on top of hers. "It is funny, shortstuff. But if you think about it, we spend a lot of time together, so it stands to reason, some of that time, we would be eating."

Grinning at him, she squeezed his hand before saying, "You're right. It's just part of what we do when we're together I guess, huh?"

Encouraged that she was touching him, he laced his fingers with hers. "I like spending time with you, Tinsleigh. I'd like to spend more time with you, if you're interested."

Wait, what? He was interested in seeing her outside of the gym? "Really? I mean, are you sure?"

"Positive."

"I didn't think…that is…well, I didn't think I was your type," she finally blurted out.

"Why would you think that?" he asked, genuinely curious.

"Well, didn't you say you dated Carmen? I'm nothing like her."

"That's a good thing," he replied. "So, I was wondering something," he said.

"What?"

"Well, my younger sister is getting married in a few weeks and I might have talked about you to her. Would you be willing to go with me? Be my plus one?"

"When is it?"

"Three weeks from yesterday. Just got the invitation in the mail. Can you get the time off?"

She thought about what she had coming up. "Actually, as long as I can take my laptop, I'm okay. Will we still be able to work out? My personal trainer might get upset if I stop working out."

"Yes, we can still work out. I would hate for you to get on your trainer's bad side," he joked.

"Then yes, I'd love to go with you."

After breakfast, they dropped off her fair entries then drove around the area. Seeing a huge tent, she said, "Oh! Can we stop? I've been thinking about adopting an animal."

He pulled into the parking lot where a large adoption event was going on and helped her out. "What were you thinking of getting?" he asked.

"I want a dog, but love cats as well," she replied as she peered into a cage where a dog and two cats were curled into one another. Crouching down, she crooned, "What pretty babies you all are!" and then giggled when the dog shuffled closer and snuffed before licking her fingers through the cage. She noticed the two cats were by the dog's side and turned to the volunteer who had been avidly watching. "What's their story?" she asked.

The volunteer looked at the cage and smiled a little sadly before replying, "Their owner passed away and no one in the family wanted to take them. They've been together all their lives so we want to adopt them together but who wants three animals at once?" She watched how the young woman was with the three and hope bloomed. "Would you...would you like to go to the pet room and see how they are with you outside of the cage?"

"What do you think, Thorne?"

"It's up to you, Tinsleigh. You've got a fenced yard and a screen porch."

"Yes, please, I'd like to see if these guys like me enough to come live with me and keep me company. What are their names?"

"The dog's name is Widget, and the two cats are Brownie and Snowflake."

"Are they all males?"

"Snowflake is a female but unlike most female cats, she's extremely affectionate."

"Okay, can you direct me to the room? Or do you need help with them?"

"Just go inside the store and on the left side, you'll see a bunch of rooms with benches. I'll meet you in there in a few minutes with this crew, okay?"

"Sounds good." As she went to stand, she felt his hands beneath her armpits and a slight shiver stole through her body. Turning, she smiled and said, "Thanks, Thorne, for the assist."

He followed her into the store and shook his head when she asked him if he wanted to come inside. "Shortstuff, if they need a home, they need to bond with you first."

"Shit, I forgot to ask you if this was okay. I mean, we're in your truck after all!" she exclaimed. "I suppose you could take me home and I could grab my car."

"If you decide you want them, I have no problem with them being in the truck. That's what blankets are for and the cats would be in a carrier, right?"

"Are you sure? I know this wasn't what you planned for today."

"Positive. Now, let the lady in with your new pets."

He stood just inside the door and watched as all three animals crowded around her, the cats purring and the dog making contented grunting noises. "I'll be right back, Tinsleigh," he said as he walked away to talk to the volunteer who was watching through the window, tears streaming down her face. "You okay, miss?" he softly asked.

"What? Oh, yes. It's just that…we've had them for four months now, been to countless adoption events and there's not been one person who they've taken to like her! Several people only wanted Widget, but like I said, the former owner had them all from the time they were weaned and they're so bonded, they do everything together."

"How old are they now?" he asked her.

"Three and they're all healthy so they should have good long lives. Oh my gosh, will you look at that?" she asked, pointing to where Tinsleigh had all three animals crowding onto her lap, nuzzling.

"I think it's a given that she'll be getting them," he replied, smiling at the sight before him. "Can you tell me the kind of food you've been using? I'll go ahead and start grabbing what she's going to need while she fills out the paperwork."

She quickly told him what she had been using and he popped his head in long enough to say, "Take your time, I'm going to get a cart and get what you'll need, okay? And if your new pets will let you up, I know you have paperwork to fill out."

Grinning at him, she said, "You have no clue what this means to me. I couldn't have pets at home, but Grammy and Pawpaw had dogs and cats, and I would pretend they were mine when I stayed there."

He smiled at the look on her face and left her to go get what she would need. Two hours later, he helped her load her new little family into his truck and said, "Let's get them home."

"Thank you for stopping Thorne. I really appreciate it."

"I'm not sure who adopted who, but it looks like you're going to have the company you wanted," he replied.

Once at the house, he carried in all the supplies while she showed Widget the backyard. He had just brought in the bin she was going to use for the dog's food when he heard her murmur, "I need to see about one of those dog doors that work with a collar for you, even though I'm home most of the time."

"Would that be a good idea with the cats?" he asked, coming to stand next to her.

"Dang it, you might be right. Oh well, I'll see if I can train him with the bells like Pawpaw."

"What do you mean?"

"Oh, you put a string with bells on it on the door and train the dog to knock it if they have to go outside."

"Sounds interesting. I'm sure you'll get it figured out pretty quick. Want me to fix something to eat while you get the cats set up?" he asked.

"You don't have to do that, Thorne."

"Don't mind doing it, Tinsleigh, or I wouldn't have said anything."

"Okay then. I had a new recipe I found that I wanted to try. It's on the counter and the meat is marinating in the refrigerator."

She was getting Snowflake and Brownie's litter box set up in the laundry room when she felt a twinge on her side. *Dammit, not now. Stupid kidney stones.* With the animals all set, she went back into the kitchen and burst into laughter at the sight before her. She had found another recipe for fish and Thorne had three eager animals at his feet as he worked to complete the steps and put it in the oven. "Looks like you've got a fan club," she teased as she grabbed a bottle of water.

"I'm seeing that," he said, glancing down at the small white paw that was patting his leg. "Hey, Snowflake, you can't have this, but I know your new mom bought wet food. How about if she gets you guys some of that?"

Going over to the bags still on the table, she pulled out a can of wet food and the new bowls. "Let me get these washed and I'll hook you guys right up." Within minutes, she had their wet food and a bowl of dry food set up on the new placemat. "Widget, you get to eat dinner shortly," she told the little dog. He was a cute thing, kind of short and somewhat stocky. He wagged his tail at her words and she bent down and ruffled his fur behind his ears, earning her a doggie groan.

"While dinner is cooking, do you want to sit out on the deck?" she asked.

"That sounds good to me. Let me set the timer."

Sitting on the deck, they chatted about the upcoming week. "Now, since we were so active this weekend, you don't have to come to the gym until Tuesday," he told her. He could see she was sitting somewhat stiffly and worried that the bike ride the day before had been too much too soon. "Are you feeling okay?"

"Hmm, yes, just those pesky kidney stones letting me know they're still there, I guess," she replied as she sipped her water.

"Anything you can take to help?" he asked.

"I've got some pain medicine and I'll take it in a little while. It knocks me out."

"Let me go check on dinner. You stay put. If it's ready, I'll get it plated and bring it out, okay?"

She smiled at him. He always seemed to go out of his way for her and it hadn't gone unnoticed. "That sounds wonderful to me. Thank you." He left and went back in the house, leaving her with her three new pets. "So, guys, it's just us now. What do you think of your new home?" Widget's tail thumped as he moved to where she was sitting. "Hey, Widget. You're such a handsome boy, aren't you?" The dog, now excited at her tone, was dancing around with his tongue lolling out, making him look like he was smiling. Laughing, she patted the chaise lounge and he jumped up and immediately crawled up her body to snuggle in with a sigh. She closed her eyes against the tears that threatened as the little dog relaxed in her arms. "I know you miss your old family, but I promise to love all three of you as long as you're alive."

He came back out with two plates, as well as two more bottles of water, and saw her dozing in the lounger with all three animals curled on and around her. Smiling at the picture they made, he quietly put the plates on the table before he took out his phone and snapped a picture. "Tinsleigh?" he softly called out. "Dinner's ready, shortstuff."

She woke up with a start and immediately blushed. "I can't believe I fell asleep like I did!" she exclaimed. Looking at the pets sleeping in her lap, she gently nudged them, saying, "Come on guys, momma's got to eat and you can't be on my lap for that." With grumbles from Widget and a stern-sounding meow from the cats, she soon had a clear lap. She turned and saw Thorne grabbing the plates and said, "Thank you" as he handed her one of them before sitting down.

They ate in companionable silence for a few minutes before Thorne finally spoke. "I don't know where you're finding these recipes, but I definitely want a copy of this one."

"Oh! I did a google search and printed off all the ones that sounded remotely interesting. Honestly? I forgot how much I enjoyed cooking. My ex didn't like what I made so I stopped not long after we were married."

"What did you eat?" he asked, curiosity now roused.

"Mostly take-out from his preferred restaurants. I hated it and whenever he was out of town for work, I would eat what *I* wanted to eat, whether that was something I cooked or a bowl of ice cream."

He started laughing, picturing her being defiant whenever possible. "You've got a feisty side, Tinsleigh."

Sighing, she looked at him and then replied, "Paige says I lost it for a long time, but it's coming back, apparently."

"I didn't say I didn't like it," he told her. While she hadn't really shared much about her ex, he was getting a picture of how she had lived, and he suspected that she had done what she could to avoid making waves. "Don't hold your sass from me." *Because the sassier you get, the more I want you.*

They finished their meal and she took his plate into the kitchen where she quickly cleaned up. Turning, she caught him almost behind her. "Oh! I didn't know you were right there!"

He gripped her arms to steady her. "I was coming in to help after I made sure the animals were in the house, but you got it all done."

"Yeah, there wasn't much to do."

Seeing her wince again, he said, "I'm going to go, Tinsleigh, so you can take something, okay?"

She nodded and he saw gratitude wash over her face. "I think I need to do that, yeah."

Walking to the front door, he held back doing what he wanted to do, which was pull her close and kiss her. *It will be on her timeframe, not yours, old man!* Instead, he gently squeezed her arm and leaned in to place a chaste kiss on her forehead. "I enjoyed today, Tinsleigh. We definitely have to go to the fair once it's opened so I can see the ribbons you're going to win."

She shook her head at his words. "Yes, we can go, although there are many others who are far more talented than I am."

"Hmm, don't think so. Remember, I saw what you submitted. Now, lock up and go take your medicine and I'll see you on Tuesday, okay?"

"I will. Thank you for today, Thorne. In fact, the whole weekend. I really enjoyed myself."

"I did too. Have a good evening, shortstuff."

Chapter Six

"Nine one one, what's your emergency?" the dispatcher asked.

"I...I think I need to go to the ER," she gasped out, the pain doubling her up.

"What seems to be going on, miss?"

"I think a kidney stone is trying to pass, I don't know. I'm in horrible pain and live alone, I can't drive myself."

"I'm dispatching an ambulance now, are you able to get to the door to let them in?"

"No, I can't move from the floor. I have a code to get into my door, it's one-six-eight-one," she told the dispatcher.

"Someone will be there soon," the dispatcher advised. "Do you need me to stay on the line with you until they get there?"

"I don't...I don't think so."

Disconnecting the call, she sent a text to Paige before allowing the pain to drag her into unconsciousness.

Tuesday morning

He blew out a breath in frustration as he went over the latest client's forms. Their doctor had referred them to him and he had emailed the forms so he could get an idea of what he was working with, only this individual had half-assed filled them out. Picking up the phone, he placed a call to the man and was soon engrossed in getting his answers.

"Hey, boss-man, have you seen or heard from Paige or Tinsleigh?" Izzy asked, standing in the door of the office.

He glanced up and then looked at his watch, startled to see it was after eleven. Raising his hand, he grabbed his phone to see if he had missed a call or text from either of the women.

"No, I haven't and it's not like them to miss a session," he replied.

"I would have been in sooner, but I've been dealing with the pool repairman all morning. I'm sorry."

"Not on you, Izzy, but obviously, something's wrong if neither of them showed up. I'm going over to check," he stated, grabbing his keys and phone. "If you need me, call."

"Will do. I hope everything's okay, Thorne."

"Me too."

He tried calling her on the drive to her house and it went straight to voicemail. Reaching her house, he got out and was able to see that her vehicle was in the garage. *What in the hell was going on?* He rang the doorbell while knocking and all he got for his efforts was Widget barking. Blowing out a huff of breath in frustration, he was about to go back to the office and call the local hospital when an older model sedan pulled into the driveway and shut off.

"Hello, can I help you, young man?" the older woman asked as she got out of the car.

"Maybe, I don't know. I'm looking for Tinsleigh," he replied.

"And you are?" she asked, reaching him where he still stood on the porch.

"My apologies. I'm Thorne Baker. I'm Tinsleigh's personal trainer. She and her friend didn't show up this morning and when I couldn't reach her by phone, I came over to make sure everything was okay."

"Oh! You're the one the girls have been talking about," she said. "I'm Abigail Timmons, Paige's mother."

"Pleasure to meet you, ma'am. Are...are they alright? I just saw Tinsleigh Sunday afternoon."

She looked up at the younger man and made a decision before replying, "Tinsleigh's kidney stone apparently decided to play rough Sunday night. She's been in the hospital ever since."

The hospital? Why didn't she call? Out loud, he said, "Mercy Hope?"

"Yes, and Paige has been with her since she got her text. I'm here to make sure the pets are okay."

He smiled remembering Sunday and how much fun they had, especially once she found the little trio of pets. "They're doing okay, aren't they? She just got them on Sunday."

"I think they're confused, but they're safe and fed and that's most important right now.

You go on, Mr. Baker, and take care of my girl, will you?"

"I plan to, Mrs. Timmons," he replied, already heading to his truck.

He walked into her hospital room and immediately went to sit next to the bed. Glancing over, he saw Paige curled up in the recliner, sleeping. He gently took Tinsleigh's hand in his, not wanting to wake her up but needing to touch her. "Oh sweetheart, why didn't you call me?" he quietly asked.

"I wanted her to, but she said it wasn't like that between the two of you," Paige replied. He looked at her and saw she was standing, motioning him to follow her. Standing up, he gently kissed the sleeping woman's forehead before he followed her friend out into the hallway.

"Why would she think that? I just told her Sunday I wanted to spend more time with her," he said.

"How much do you know about her family? Her ex?" Paige asked.

"Not that much other than she doesn't really speak to her parents since her divorce."

"C'mon, I need some coffee and we need to talk."

He followed her down to the hospital's cafeteria where they both grabbed some coffee and she got some breakfast. When she went to pay, he said, "No, I've got this, you go get a seat for us." Once he had paid the cashier, he walked over to the table she had chosen and sat.

"Okay, I think I need to clue you in a little bit about why Tiny is the way she is," Paige said.

"I'm listening." *Fuck, what had his girl gone through to make her think he wouldn't want to be by her side?*

Paige drank some of her coffee as she looked at the man sitting across from her. She had known since she joined the gym that he was interested in Tinsleigh and had told her as well, but her best friend couldn't see it. Taking a deep breath, she said, "Tiny and I met in middle school and became fast friends, doing everything together. The first time I spent the night at her house, she told me that she had never had a sleepover before. Anyhow, her house and family were completely opposite from how I grew up. The house is quite lovely, if you like rooms that look like they're not lived in but are only there for display. When we went to her room, I was blown away. Instead of a typical eleven-year old's room with posters and pictures everywhere, it was...almost sterile. The walls were a light cream color and the pictures weren't of boy bands and favorite movies. They were replicas of famous works. Anyhow, I had a good time, even though it was the housekeeper who kept us entertained. We slept down in the family room and had gourmet pizza. It was...different. And I saw how her mother treated her and talked to her. Thorne, she's never ever been good enough. Her mother has criticized every aspect of Tiny that she could – from what she wore to who she hung out with and it's honestly a miracle that she allowed us to be friends."

"How is it possible that she was allowed to continue to be friends with you if her mom was like that?" he asked. He could remember rambunctious sleepovers when he was a kid, with movies and popcorn and takeout pizza. What Paige had described sounded so foreign to him he was having a hard time wrapping his mind around what she had said to him.

"My father is the local school superintendent and Mrs. Martin felt it was a 'good' friendship for Tiny to have," she replied.

"Okay, I have another question and then I won't interrupt again," he said. "Why do you call her 'Tiny'?"

Laughing, she looked at him and said, "My little sister, Maggie, couldn't say Tinsleigh so she called her Tiny and because she's so petite, the name stuck."

He thought about the woman lying in the hospital room upstairs and agreed. She *was* petite but he knew to the depths of his heart that they would fit perfectly.

"Well, the first time she was allowed to come to *my* house, she saw the difference immediately. My family is loud and we laugh a lot and joke around. Tiny wasn't used to the easy affection that my parents gave us and at first, she was a bit standoffish. But my mom finally wore her down. You've got to understand, Thorne, that her dad isn't a bad guy. He just works all the time and travels a lot. He didn't get a lot of input into how she was raised, that was Mrs. Martin's job."

"Anyhow, she has grown up hearing that her actions reflect on the family and their reputation. Towards the end of middle school, Denny moved to town. He was one of the cutest boys in the eighth grade and because he came from the same social background that Tiny did, her mother was thrilled that he was paying attention to her. They started dating, if you could call it that, about a month after he moved to town. They dated throughout high school until our senior year. Then, he broke up with her for oh, maybe six months or so. During that time, he dated Carmen, who lorded it over Tiny."

She saw his head drop at her words. Curiously, she asked, "Thorne? Are you okay?"

"Yeah. She and I ran into Carmen over the weekend and Carmen was nasty to her, but in a very snarky way, if that makes sense."

"Oh yeah, that's how she rolls. She's a bitch on wheels and she made our lives, especially Tiny's, hell in school. Anyhow, they finally broke up and he came back to Tiny and she took him back, claiming she 'loved him'."

"I've...uh...*dated* Carmen."

"Oh, fuck," Paige muttered. "That's going to give that bitch something else to crow about whenever she sees Tiny."

"How so?"

"Well, and again, I'm telling you this because I think you genuinely care about her so *don't* fuck that up, Carmen *slept* with Denny. That was something Tiny wasn't ready to do, but Carmen was easy, so he bailed."

"What a dick," he muttered. "So, let me get this straight – her mother is a bitch and so is Carmen. What about her sisters? She mentioned she has two."

"She gets along with them to an extent, but they're carbon copies of Mrs. Martin, so they're condescending towards Tiny as well."

My poor girl. She's had no one in her corner. Well, except for Paige and her family. "How did she end up marrying him?"

"You've got to understand, she was so conditioned to accept how she was treated that when she wouldn't sleep with him because they weren't married, he proposed. Basically, he wanted in her pants."

Again, he shook his head. His *heart* hurt and he knew that it was going to take a lot to prove to Tinsleigh that he cared for her just as she was, he didn't want a robot. "What happened during their marriage?"

"Well, after the 'wedding of the century' that her parents put on, she settled into domestic living. Whatever Denny wanted to do, they did. She *lost* herself, Thorne, and it killed me to see her sinking so far into herself. She kept the perfect home, went to the places *he* wanted to go, and ignored the fact that he basically put her on a shelf. I found out, after their divorce, that he had been running around on her for most of their marriage. With Carmen, of all people. That ended when he got a new assistant. He's married to her now and they have a child. Anyhow, when he left that day, he broke her completely. For the first six months, she ate her feelings, telling me and my mom she was 'fine' even though we could tell she wasn't, not at all. Then, I think she decided she couldn't keep going on that way, so she finally put her college education to good use and really started promoting her business and began changing her habits. You kind of know the rest," she said. "I know it's a lot, but since we've started working out, my best friend is emerging. And *you're* a big part of that, whether you know it or not."

Sighing, he said, "So, in essence, I'm going to need to show her how I feel and it's likely going to take time."

"Yeah, I think so, although honestly? I've seen more of 'her' in the past month or so than I have since we were kids. I mean, she's always been real with *me* but around everyone else, she reverts to what she has been conditioned to be. Her grammy was good for her, and so was her pawpaw. I *loved* going there with her because they loved her so much and it showed in everything they said and did. The best thing they could have done for her was give her their house."

"She mentioned them and I could see how much she cared by how she talked," he told her. "Okay, now that I know that so I can be mindful, what in the hell happened that has her here?"

She motioned for him to wait and she took a long sip off her coffee. "I know you guys pretty much spent the weekend together," she said. At his raised eyebrow, she continued, "Not like *that* although, if you two keep going, I imagine it will happen. Anyhow, she had a couple of kidney stones and the doctor was hopeful that she would be able to pass them without surgery."

"She mentioned Sunday night she was having some pain. I told her to take her medicine and I would see her Tuesday," he replied. "I should have known it was worse than she let on."

"No no no. Don't blame yourself. She *did* take her medicine but sometime in the middle of the night, she woke up in excruciating pain. Thank God she took her phone into the bathroom. She thought she was passing the stone, but apparently, it got stuck. She called nine one one and managed to send me a text before she passed out."

"How did they get into the house?" he asked.

"Her house has a code access and she gave the operator the code so the paramedics could get in. They got there, she was unconscious, so they loaded her up and brought her here. I got here a few minutes after she did and was able to tell them what was going on. They did surgery early Monday morning and she's pretty much been knocked out ever since."

"Did...did they have to cut her open?" he asked.

"No, it's some sort of procedure where they're basically pounding on the kidney with ultrasound waves to bust them up so they *can* pass. That's why she's sleeping now. It's pretty painful and they will keep her medicated for a few days until the worst has passed."

"Did she tell you I invited her to be my date for my sister's wedding?"

"Yes, she did. She's kind of nervous about meeting your sister because she said y'all are really close."

"Gloria is going to love her."

"Okay, I want to get back up there, are you coming?" she asked as she stood.

"I'll be back shortly. I'm thinking my girl needs some flowers to show her she's important," he replied.

"She also loves those crafting magazines," Paige advised.

He chuckled. "How has she been eating while she's been here?"

"She said the food is terrible, so she hasn't really eaten much."

"Okay, then I'll run to the diner we've eaten at and grab her something. Do you want me to get you something as well? I noticed you hardly touched what you got."

She looked down at the half-full plate and laughed. "Yeah. Whatever you get Tiny is fine with me."

"Then I'll be back shortly, okay? Don't tell her I've already been here once."

"I won't. It'll be a surprise when you get back!" she said, laughing at the look on his face. He was a man on a mission now and her heart cheered for her best friend, knowing that the man in front of her was going to be everything to her and more once he broke through her wall.

He stopped at the local florist shop and looked around until he found the perfect thing – tulips that she could replant outside once they had died down. He couldn't find a card he liked, so he paid for the flowers and headed to the drugstore, where he found the perfect card as well as several quilting magazines he thought she would enjoy. Back in the truck, he drove to the diner and went in to place three to-go orders. While he waited, he wrote on the inside of the card. Once the meals were bagged up and he had paid, he headed back to the hospital.

Walking back into her room, he stopped and stared. She was awake and chatting with Paige but when she saw him, she smiled, saying, "Hey, Thorne, what are you doing here?"

He put the plant down, handed her the card and the magazines and pulled out the food, putting her container on her table and making sure she could reach everything before he replied. "Well, when I realized you were late this morning, I went by your house and ran into Mrs. Timmons who told me you were here. I came by a bit ago but you were sleeping so Paige and I chatted and then, when she said that you didn't like the food, I went and got you some."

She looked at the plant and the card and the magazines and replied, "I think you did a little more than that! Thank you."

"How are you feeling?"

"Sore, very sore. The good news is, they got them all busted up and they've passed. Plus, Dr. Day said that with my lifestyle changes, it's unlikely that I'll be dealing with them again. She also said that she could see how much of a difference the time we've spent together has made. But I wouldn't let her tell me how much weight I've lost," she said.

He started laughing. She was adamant that she not be told her current weight and he was honoring her wishes, but he knew she had dropped weight already in just the few weeks they had begun working out.

"It's not funny, Thorne! All my life, the focus was on the *numbers* not how I felt or how I looked in clothes. I think it's wrong that people quantify others based on a damn number."

"Sweetheart, I happen to agree with you on that one. And the most important thing is you are getting healthier. The number on the scale is just a benefit, like whipped cream on hot cocoa. Now, I have a bit of a bone to pick with you."

"What…what do you mean?" she asked. When he saw the fear in her eyes, he mentally sighed at his choice of words.

Sitting down next to her, he took her hand and said, "I thought we decided on Sunday to start dating?"

She nodded, her eyes still cautious.

"Well, sweetheart, I would expect if that was the case, you would have let me know what happened. I sure as hell would have been here sooner if I had known."

"You...you would have?"

Remember, she doesn't think she has any value other than as an object in someone's life. "Yeah, Tinsleigh, I would have been here for you. You matter to me, a great deal, and while I have no idea where this is headed," *liar-liar his conscience taunted, "I* want you to understand that something this important is a big deal to me too."

He saw the relief on her face and knew that somehow, her ex had let her down in the past so she had thought to protect herself by not telling him she was in the hospital. "Now, how about we all eat before it gets cold?"

With that, all three began eating. When his phone chimed, he glanced at it and saw that Izzy had texted him. He responded and then said, "That was Izzy. She was worried when she didn't hear back from me. I told her briefly what was going on so don't be surprised if she shows up at some point."

"She's become a friend, Thorne, so I don't mind. The three of us are planning a girl's night out soon, as a matter of fact."

The nurse came in as they were finishing their lunches and said, "Ah, look at you, getting this good-looking man to get you something edible to eat! I need to check your vitals and it's time for more of your pain medicine, so it's good that you've eaten."

"He's taking good care of me now that he knows where I'm at," Tinsleigh said, smiling at the man who was sitting as close as he could to her hospital bed.

"I can see that! Food, magazines *and* flowers? Girl, you hit the mother lode," the nurse said as she got ready to inject the medicine into the IV. "You're probably going to get drowsy again."

"Rest's important, sweetheart," he interjected when he saw her start to shake her head. "I don't mind sitting here with you while you sleep."

"I'm sure you've got better things to do than watch me sleep," she replied.

"Hmm, not that I'm aware of, so rest. The sooner you do what they say, the sooner you can get home to Widget, Snowflake and Brownie."

She squeezed his hand and let the medicine work. As she slept, he and Paige talked quietly and he finally asked, "Did you let her parents know?"

"She didn't want me to, said that it would be an inconvenience to her mother."

"Maybe let her dad know? I gather they're somewhat close?"

"They are, as much as can be with his work schedule. She tries to meet him once a week for lunch, so I probably should let him know," she replied, grabbing Tinsleigh's phone. He watched as she opened up the text messages and found the one she was looking for before she quickly sent a text. Finished, she looked at him and said, "I bet anything, he calls."

Minutes later, Tinsleigh's phone rang and she answered it. While he could only hear her half of the conversation, he quickly figured out that she had filled him in on what was going on with his daughter. After she hung up, she looked at Thorne and said, "We better prepare for the invasion. There's no way he'll show up without her mother."

"What do you mean, prepare for them?" he asked, curiosity now roused.

"I need to run to her house and get an appropriate nightgown so I can help her shower."

"Her dad's that bad?"

"It's not her dad, it's her mother."

"No," he said.

"No?"

"Absolutely not. She's in pain and doesn't need to stand up and shower for *anyone*. She is fine in her hospital gown and you already got her a brush, right? As long as her hair is brushed, her mother can go pound salt."

"I knew you would be good for her," Paige said, smiling.

"*She's* good for me," he replied.

"Oh sweetheart, I wish you had called me," a male voice said next to the hospital bed. Thorne's eyes opened from his doze and he saw a middle-aged man standing on the other side of Tinsleigh's bed, smoothing back her hair.

"She didn't tell anyone," he said. "I'm Thorne Baker, her boyfriend," he replied in response to the man's raised eyebrows. "I didn't find out until I met Mrs. Timmons at her house."

"Why was she at Tinsleigh's house?"

"She was taking care of her pets for her."

"Tinsleigh has pets now?"

"In all fairness, she just adopted them last weekend so they're new. Well, not new-new, but she adopted a trio of pets whose owner had passed away because they were bonded and she didn't want them separated."

The older man chuckled before saying, "That sounds like her. She always wanted pets as a little girl but her mother has allergies."

"I see," Thorne replied.

"How is she feeling? Is she in a lot of pain?" her dad asked. "By the way, I'm Graham Martin."

He took the proffered hand and shook it. It seemed the older man was trying and for that, he'd give him some leeway. "She's in some pain, but they were able to do the non-invasive procedure so she should be back to normal in a few days once the rest of the broken pieces pass."

"Does she need anything? Has anyone let her clients know?"

"I sent out an email this morning from her phone," Paige said. "She's current on everything right now and if anyone really needs anything, I'll bring her laptop up."

"No," Thorne said.

"But, she needs to…" Paige started.

"She needs to rest. Her clients should understand a medical emergency," he replied.

Graham Martin looked at the younger man sitting by his daughter. He was generally good at reading people and liked what he saw and what he was hearing. Seemed that she got a good one this time around, unlike that dickhead, Denny. He knew that his wife had given her hell for the divorce, but he also knew that it wasn't her fault. He just wished he could get Martine to see that she had driven their daughter away with her behavior. "I agree with him, Paige. She works hard and I'm sure she'll be able to catch up pretty quickly once she's home."

"Daddy?" Tinsleigh asked, her voice raspy. "What…what are you doing here?"

"Why wouldn't I come and check on my favorite oldest daughter when I find out she had to have surgery?" he replied as he bent down and kissed her forehead. "How are you feeling, honey?"

"A little sore but the doctor said that was to be expected. I…I won't be able to make lunch tomorrow, I guess."

"How about if I bring it to you?" he asked.

She smiled at him. Since they had started meeting for lunch, she had developed a stronger bond with him and he had apologized to her for letting her mother run roughshod over her. "I would like that a lot," she replied softly.

"Other than that, I wanted to tell you that you look marvelous."

"It's all thanks to Thorne," she said.

"No, shortstuff, it's because you're putting in the hard work," Thorne interjected. "Although to be fair, I thought you looked beautiful before you started working out."

She looked at him and he could see the shock on her face. He knew from talking to Paige that Denny had grown more and more critical of her looks. *Another wall to break down.* "I'm serious, Tinsleigh. Your body type is more of an hourglass and speaking for myself, I prefer a woman that is happy in her own skin, regardless of her size."

Graham looked at the younger man once again, liking what he was hearing. He knew how his wife had badgered their daughter about her weight, claiming no one would ever want her. He had many regrets about his role as a father and that was one of them. His beautiful daughter had slowly disappeared over the years, only to be replaced by a woman who worried about everything.

Seeing her now with this man, he realized that she was starting to come back to who she was when she was younger, only now she had the maturity of an adult. And he liked what he saw.

"I'm going to have to agree with him, Tinsleigh. You remind me a lot of your grandmother in your looks and mannerisms."

"I miss Grammy," she replied.

"I do too. How is the house? Any more renovations?" he asked. It had been a few years since he had visited the house. Martine was still livid that his parents had willed it and a small inheritance to Tinsleigh, but he knew that his parents were trying to make sure that she always had somewhere to go.

"Well, I finally got the back porch screened in so I could hang out there and read. Now that I have Widget, Snowflake and Brownie, I think it'll be my favorite room. You should come and see, Daddy."

"How about once you get home?" he asked.

"I'd like that a lot."

"Okay, what do you want for lunch tomorrow?"

She thought for a moment then motioned for Paige to hand over her phone. Pulling up the website of the deli they frequented, she looked at the menu and then said, "Can you pick something up from Delrados? If so, I'd love the salmon pita, some braised white beans and maybe a piece of that yummy chocolate cake?"

Thorne started laughing at the side look she had given him. "Sweetheart, I told you, it's a lifestyle change, so you can eat things you enjoy. From what I gathered, you really haven't eaten much the past few days anyhow, so a piece of cake won't hurt."

"Would either of you like something?" Graham asked.

Thorne shook his head before saying, "I have a new client coming to the gym tomorrow."

"And I am going to come by later, Tiny," Paige replied. "Thanks anyway, Mr. Martin."

Thorne sighed in frustration. The new client was driving him crazy and he wasn't sure how to break through to him. "Look, Jonathan, I'm willing to help you but you've got to do the work."

"I appreciate it, but it's been years since I worked out."

"It will come back to you. How are you doing with the eating plan?"

"It's been hard, not gonna lie, but I have two choices – lose the weight or end up having bypass surgery like my old man did."

"Then you need to buckle down." Hearing his phone chime, he said, "Excuse me, I need to get it."

"No problem. I'm heading to the pool."

Going into his office, he sat down before looking at his phone.

Tinsleigh: Hey are you busy? I've got octopus mobbing the floor.

He looked at the text, puzzled at the message. Her texts were sometimes a bit crazy and she blamed it on her use of voice to text.

Thorne: I thought you didn't like tentacles?
Tinsleigh: What? Oh for heaven's sakes, I just read what I sent you. Sigh.
Thorne: Voice to text again?
Tinsleigh: LOL. Um, yeah. I meant to say I get to go home. Siri obviously hates me.

He burst into laughter. While he had decided she would set the pace regarding when they would go further, they had spent a lot of time since she was in the hospital talking. He had finally told her about his brother and his ex, figuring she needed to know the dynamics before they headed to his sister's wedding. He still remembered how angry she had gotten not only at Roger but also at Marisa.

Thorne: How soon will you be ready to go? I can come and get you.
Tinsleigh: Paige is here and will bring me home, I know you're working.
Thorne: Can I come by after work?
Tinsleigh: I'd like that. I'll cook.
Thorne: No, I'll cook.
Thorne: I know you're rolling your eyes, but I want you to rest.
Tinsleigh: I'm not going to win, am I?
Thorne: Nope. I'll pick stuff up on my way over, okay?
Tinsleigh: Fine. See you when you get there.
Thorne: Later shortstuff.

He put his phone down and went back into the gym, smiling. She was slowly healing his heart and didn't have a clue.

"C'mon, girlie, let's blow this popsicle stand," Paige said as she came into the room. "I've got clean clothes if you want to shower here or we can just wait until we get to your house."

"I just want to get home, so I'll wait," Tinsleigh replied.

"Well, Mom is there now, and she's likely going to want to play nursemaid so be prepared," Paige said, laughing.

"I'm good with that to be honest. I feel like I went through a fifteen-round fight and lost."

"Dr. Day said that will ease up once the rest of the pieces pass."

"I know, I just hate that I feel so damn weak. I'm ready to work out again, my body is craving it now."

"You know Thorne's going to be watching you like a hawk. How's that going, by the way?"

She smiled at her friend. "It's going well. I mean, we *still* haven't kissed but he told me that I was setting the pace and until I was ready, he would wait. What kind of man does that?"

"A good one. And, from what you told me about his past, one that has been burned. I think he wants to make sure you know what you want."

"Him. I want him. He's the first person outside of you and your family who accepts me just as I am, warts and all."

"Tiny, I know it's early days for you two, but I think he's 'the one' for you," Paige said as she gathered the things so they could leave.

"You might be right, my friend. I've never felt like this with anyone, even Denny."

"Well, Denny was always an asshole, so I can understand why you didn't feel like that with him."

"He wasn't that..." she started to say.

"Don't you *dare* say he wasn't that bad! Holy hell, Tiny, that man had to 'approve' of every aspect of your life!"

"I know, you're right. I can't believe I didn't see it before now though."

"You didn't see it because that's what you've been conditioned to receive. Your mom is the same way if you think about it," Paige replied.

"Yeah, you're right. I mean, she never even called to check on me and I know Daddy told her where I was," she said. "I mean, who doesn't check on their own child when they've been told they had surgery?" she asked, almost rhetorically. They both knew how her mother was and her behavior wasn't surprising in the least. Hurtful to an extent, but not surprising. "Your mom has been at my house every day, twice a day, taking care of the new zoo crew *and* she still managed to come and see me too!"

"She loves you, Tiny," Paige replied. Mrs. Martin was a real piece of work and she would never understand how she couldn't be happy to have a daughter as awesome as Tiny. "Alright, let's go, girlie."

"Mama Tee, I can't thank you enough for helping with these guys," Tinsleigh said as she sat on the recliner couch, surrounded by her pets. "They look happy and content."

"You know you don't have to thank me. You're like one of my own," the older woman said as she fussed around Tinsleigh. "Now, pop up that recliner and get some rest.

I'm sure these three won't be leaving your side any time soon."

She knew she wouldn't win any argument, so she extended the recliner and leaned back with a sigh. The trip home had been exhausting and after a light lunch, Mama Tee had made her take a pain pill. As she started to doze, she felt a throw being placed around her and she snuggled in, allowing the contented purrs of the cats and occasional grunt from the dog to lull her into a restful, healing sleep.

He lightly knocked on the door and wasn't surprised when Mrs. Timmons opened it with her finger to her lips. Walking inside, he saw the woman who made his heart race sleeping in the recliner, surrounded by her new pet family. He followed the older woman into the kitchen and sat at the table when she motioned him to do so. "How is she doing?" he finally asked.

"I think she's just tired. They got home and she showered and then I fed her. The ride was a bit hard because of the construction so she just took a pain pill maybe thirty minutes ago."

"Ah okay, so she'll likely sleep for a bit. I told her I would cook tonight, so that gives me time to run and grab a few things," he replied.

"She mentioned you were going to cook when I offered," Mrs. Timmons said. "I'm fine either way. Why don't you check the fridge before you head out, there may be something here?"

"Good idea. I should have stopped on my way over, but I wanted to get here."

"She's important to you, isn't she?"

"Yeah, she is, more than she realizes. That's the hard part for me – how can she not know just how special she is?"

Mrs. Timmons sighed. She knew Paige had told him how Tinsleigh was raised, as well as how her ex treated her. "She's just so conditioned, Thorne," she told him. "But since she's been working out with you, I have seen more of the young girl that I first met than I have in many years."

"We're both good for one another," he told the older woman. "Let me see what she has available before I go and pick anything up," he said as he went to the freezer. His grin widened when he saw how she had set up her freezer with meats that were separated with possible recipe ideas written on the outside of the containers. *Variety. She likes variety.*

Pulling out two packages of steak to thaw, he then checked the fridge and saw she had asparagus. "Okay, I need to run and pick a few things up to put a salad together. Anything else you think she'd want or need?" he asked, grabbing the pad of paper from the front of the refrigerator and sitting back down. He quickly jotted the few items he wanted to get onto the list and then looked expectantly at Mrs. Timmons.

"She really likes that dreamsicle-flavored ice cream," Mrs. Timmons said.

He nodded. His woman had a bit of a sweet tooth which made him smile. She was figuring out how to work her likes into her eating plan. "Then I'll be sure to grab her some. Anything else?"

"I don't think so. You two got everything for the pets and they're still set, so other than the water she seems to like now and what you put on the list, she should be set."

"Then I'll be back shortly," he replied, standing and walking over to where she was still sleeping. Leaning down, he gently kissed her forehead and murmured, "Be back in a bit, Tins."

Chapter Seven

She woke up to the smell of something wonderful cooking and tried to stretch, only to find herself pinned in by the three bundles of fur. "Hey guys," she whispered, reaching down and petting each of them in turn. "I need to get up and use the bathroom." When none of them moved, she started to giggle at her predicament.

"What's so funny?" Thorne asked, coming back into the family room.

"I uh, I have to get up and go to the bathroom and these guys are saying 'no way, lady, we ain't letting you leave'," she replied.

"Let me give you a hand then," he said. "C'mon, Widget, let's go outside." When the little dog snuffled before standing and stretching, he continued, saying, "Good boy. Let your momma get up." Within seconds, all three animals had moved, and he leaned in to offer his hand.

"I can get up," she protested as he all but picked her up.

"I know, just making sure you're steady. Come out to the kitchen when you're done and keep me company."

"Okay."

She took care of business then looked at herself in the mirror as she was washing her hands. "Ugh, I look like a hot mess!" she muttered out loud, seeing the dark circles under her eyes. And yet, he hadn't treated her any differently. *Hmm, if it had been Denny, he would have made a few comments by now. Then again, Thorne isn't Denny and he's shown me that many times already. Time to get rid of those thoughts, girlie!*

Going back into her room, she laughed when she saw the three animals waiting for her. "C'mon, guys, let's go keep Thorne company, shall we?" she asked as she headed out of the room and back toward the kitchen.

"I see you've got your posse," he said as she walked into the kitchen. "Here, sit down and I'll grab you something to drink."

"Thank you. I'm supposed to move to help the stuff they used dissipate, though," she told him as she sat at the table.

"And there's time enough for that later. I thought we could take Widget for a walk after we eat if you're up to it," he replied, sitting a glass filled with her favorite diet soda.

"Oh, this is so good," she said as she took a sip. "I've been trying to limit how much I drink of it with the stones."

"I know, but I checked with the doctor and she said it was okay if you had some occasionally."

"So, what's for dinner?" she asked, watching him move around her kitchen as if he lived there. *I like how he looks in my kitchen!*

"Flank steak with a ginger marinade, Italian green beans, asparagus, and a baked potato."

"Sounds delicious."

"And I picked up some of the ice cream you enjoy."

"Dreamsicle?"

He burst into laughter. "Yes, ma'am."

Within minutes, he had the food served and they sat down to eat. "The doctor said you need to take it easy for a few days," he said.

Nodding, she replied, "I know, but now that I've started working out, I hate to lose any momentum."

"Let's give it a day or two, then you can get in and walk the pool. The resistance will still give you a workout, but it won't put too much strain on you while you're healing."

She sighed before asking, "What about the treadmill?"

"No more than twenty minutes."

"Thorne, that's not going to help me," she stated.

"You're so far ahead of where most others would be right now, you can afford an easy week. Besides, you can walk Widget and we can also adjust some things and focus on upper body work."

"Okay."

"But…I'll be watching you like a hawk so don't think you can push too hard too soon," he cautioned.

"I'm okay with that," she replied, trying and failing to hide the grin that spread across her face.

"You've got some smooth level ground to walk on around here," he said. "I'm kind of surprised."

"Years ago, when my pawpaw was building the house, he paid to have the sidewalk put in on either side so we could eventually get to the other houses. As each one was built on the road, the homeowner added to it until each side had sidewalks. I don't know how they managed to do it except we're out in the country, but then again, Pawpaw had a way of getting folks to agree with him when he felt something needed to be done."

"He sounds awesome. Wish I could have known him," he said as they walked Widget back toward the house.

"He really was. They both taught me so much and I miss them dearly," she replied. The walk had done her some good, but she could tell with the ache she was feeling that it was a good thing they were headed back to her house.

"You're starting to hurt," he said, watching as she changed how she was walking.

"A little bit, yeah," she confessed.

"Let's get you back in and settled. I'm going to stay in case you need anything."

"You don't have to do that," she stated as they walked up the sidewalk to the porch.

"It's okay. Paige plans to be here in the morning after she works out and then I'll head to the gym."

"I don't need anyone babysitting me!" she exclaimed.

"Tins, let us take care of you, please?" he asked as he unclipped Widget's leash and hung it up.

"Fine," she said. He grinned because he could hear the huffiness in her voice.

"Why don't you go get into something more comfortable and we can watch a movie?" he asked. "It's too early for either of us to go to bed and I want to feel you curled up next to me for a bit."

She looked at him and could see the desire he was trying to mask. He had told her repeatedly that everything that happened between them would happen at *her* pace and her respect for him grew. Nodding, she headed toward her room and totally missed him muttering, "Even if it kills me."

"Here," he said, handing her a bowl with her favorite ice cream in it.

"Isn't popcorn the standard movie snack?" she asked, taking the bowl and spoon he held out.

"Yeah, but I figured you would want something sweet first," he replied as he settled in next to her before pulling up the handle so they were reclined. "I really like this couch you have, there's plenty of room for us both right here."

"It's definitely roomy," she said, spooning some of the creamy orange deliciousness into her mouth. "No, Widget, you have to wait," she told the little brown dog as he attempted to jump up next to her. "Momma's eating and you aren't allowed near me for that, little man." The dog gave her a mournful look before plopping down on his stomach, grumbling the whole time. "If I didn't know better, I'd think he was telling me off," she stated, looking at Thorne.

He started laughing. "I think he's playing you, sweetheart. He'll be fine while we enjoy our treat. Once we're done, I'll make us some air popcorn and grab a couple of sodas. He can have some popcorn and it won't hurt him."

While she enjoyed her ice cream he watched her, seeing the circles under her eyes from the pain and lack of good sleep. Vowing to himself to make sure she got better, he took her empty bowl and said, "Be right back. Grab the remote and let's see what we can find to watch."

With Halloween around the corner, she found "Hocus Pocus" on Netflix and when he came back in with a bowl of popcorn and two sodas, she said, "How's this? It's about the only Halloween movie I can handle except Charlie Brown's 'It's the Great Pumpkin, Charlie Brown' because I just don't like scary stuff."

Laughing, he settled next to her, handing her the bowl while he opened up the recliner before reclaiming the bowl and putting it on his lap. She blushed a little, having seen what he was attempting to hide with the bowl. *I never affected Denny like that and dayum, he's packing a serious weapon to boot!*

"So, what do I need to wear for the wedding?" she asked.

"Gloria is having a Halloween theme – oranges and black and that deep green, I think," he replied, his hand now idly playing with her curls. "So, I guess a fall colored dress? I'm sure you and Paige will find something."

She started laughing because in the short time they'd known him, he had figured out that she and Paige had no problems shopping for things that were needed. "Yeah, I'll hit her up and see when she wants to go shopping."

She woke up slowly, aware that she was laying on his lap against a very impressive erection. Widget was wedged behind her and the cats were on her side underneath the throw that he must have pulled over her. Thorne's arm was curled possessively around her waist, giving her a warm and cozy feeling deep inside. *Never felt like this before. Ever. Now to fix my fucked-up head so I can be what this wonderful man needs.*

"Thorne?" she whispered, her voice raspy with sleep. "We...we fell asleep."

He woke up with a start at her words. "I see the pet posse got in on it too," he murmured, looking at how the three had wedged themselves around her. "C'mon guys, time to get down." Widget lifted his head and grumbled, but got off the couch, followed by Snowflake and Brownie. "Let's get you up so you can get to bed," he said, helping her to sit upright. Seeing the tent in his lounge pants had him internally cringing, but whenever she was around that was his normal state of affairs. She stood and stretched, her pajama top pulling across her chest and he bit back a groan. This waiting was going to kill him, but he *would* wait until she gave the signal. *Please let it be soon.*

"I'm going to put him out one last time. Do you need to take anything?" he asked, standing and trying to discreetly adjust himself. Damn lounge pants, they hid nothing. What he didn't realize was that him being turned-on was a healing balm to her soul.

"Yeah, I need to take a pain pill. Being in one position and having the cats laying on the side where they did surgery has me hurting a bit."

He held out his hand and they walked into the kitchen, where he let Widget out and refreshed the water bowl for the animals while she got a bottle of water and quickly took a pain pill. "I'll make sure everything is locked up. You go on to bed," he said, coming over and kissing her forehead. "Sleep well, shortstuff. I'll see you in the morning."

"G'night, Thorne," she murmured, still sleepy. "Thank you for tonight."

"My pleasure."

She woke up to the chiming of her phone. Grabbing it from the nightstand, she saw it was Paige.

Paige: Wakey wakey, time for eggs and bakey!

Tinsleigh: Really? You're killing me!

Paige: I should be there soon. Whatcha want to do?

Tinsleigh: I don't know. We have to shop for a dress for the wedding I'm going to.

Paige: Shopping? Can you handle that today?

Tinsleigh: Don't see why not.

Paige: Fine. We'll go out to breakfast then hit the stores.

Tinsleigh: See you soon.

Getting out of bed, she was happy to see she didn't hurt as much as the day before. Grinning, she grabbed leggings and an oversized t-shirt before heading into the shower. As she stood under the spray, she thought about the man staying in her guest bedroom. He was everything she had always dreamed of in a man – looks aside, he was generous, caring, and patient. Of course, the looks didn't hurt, and she felt the inner shivers at what it would be like to be held by him and loved on. *Keep being patient Thorne, I'm getting there.*

"Good morning, Tinsleigh," he said as she walked into the kitchen.

"Morning, Thorne," she replied, going to the refrigerator and grabbing some juice. "Paige is on her way over."

"What kind of plans do you have?" he asked, pouring himself a cup of coffee. She wasn't a coffee drinker, but she had a Keurig for the tea and occasional hot chocolate she enjoyed. When she found out he drank coffee, she picked some up, a fact he filed away.

"We're going to go eat breakfast and then shop for my dress."

"Just don't wear yourself out," he cautioned.

"I promise I won't. She's going to drive and I'll take my pain medicine. I can break it in half if I need to so I'm not completely knocked out."

"That's good. I pulled out some chicken to grill tonight."

"You know you don't have to be here," she told him.

"Until I know you're at one hundred percent, you're stuck with me," he replied.

"I'll put together a salad and we can have grilled chicken salads if you want," she said. "I found a recipe for raspberry vinaigrette dressing I want to try, too."

"Sounds good to me. I'm going to grab some corn on the cob as well."

Her stomach rumbled and she grinned. "Hope Paige hurries up and gets here. All this talk of food has my stomach ready."

He pulled her into a hug and felt her stiffen. Gently rubbing her back, he murmured, "Still at your pace, Tins. Just needed to give you a hug is all." He heard her sigh as she relaxed. *Damn she fits me perfectly.* Placing a kiss on the top of her head, he said, "Gotta get to the gym. My newest client needs a swift kick in the ass."

"That bad, huh?"

"He's just having a hard time adjusting to everything. Maybe once he sees how you and Paige work out, he'll get with the program."

She laughed and said, "Yeah, if he's got any male pride, he's not going to want two women to show him up. We'll be there tomorrow so I can do a light workout."

"I'll call Dr. Day and find out what you can and cannot do," he advised. "You're going to be back in time for your dad to come by, aren't you?"

"We should be, yes. I kind of have an idea of the dress I want and that won't take long since I know I'm still supposed to 'take it easy' this week," she replied. "But I'll call him to let him know as well so he doesn't come early."

"See you later, sweetheart," he said, coming over and kissing her forehead. "You and Paige try to keep yourselves out of trouble."

"What's the fun in that?" she asked, laughing.

He just shook his head as he grabbed his keys by the front door and headed out, nearly running into Paige.

"Hey, Thorne! I managed to get a workout in before I headed here," she said, her slightly damp hair giving testament to her claim.

"Good. You two have fun this morning. Don't let her do too much," he replied.

"I promise I won't," she told him.

Chapter Eight

"Girl, that man is *fine*," Paige said once he had left.

"Don't I know it," Tinsleigh replied, putting her shoes on. "You ready? He started talking about food and my stomach began growling."

"Uh, yeah. I put in a good workout this morning so let's hit the road."

"We'll need to run by the grocery store on our way back, too. He's grilling chicken tonight and we're making salads with it, so I have to pick up a few things."

"We can do that, absolutely."

As they drove to their favorite diner for breakfast, they chatted about her upcoming trip to his dad's house for his sister's wedding. "I'm a bit nervous, to be honest."

"Why?" Paige asked as she pulled into a parking spot.

"Because he told me what his ex did and there's a good possibility she'll be there," Tinsleigh admitted, getting out of the car.

"So? I'm telling you, he's interested in *you* and she doesn't hold a candle to the woman you are," Paige replied once they got settled in a booth.

"How can you know that? You don't even know her," Tinsleigh said, grabbing a menu.

"Because you're you, Tiny. He's just waiting on you to get with the program."

She sighed. "I need to get rid of the rest of this fucked-up thinking I've got about myself."

"You've got a false belief system about yourself is all. Time for us to uproot that bullshit and plant in some truth."

Tinsleigh started laughing at her friend's statement. "Like what?"

"Let's see – that you have no value or worth other than how you look. That you have nothing to offer to anyone relationship-wise. That you're not good enough. Those are the top three."

She thought about what Paige had said. Her mother's voice needed to be overridden – but how? And as for Denny's, well, his was a parrot of her mother, so once she got rid of that tape that played like a loop at times, she felt like his words that whispered across her soul would likely go away too. "You're right," she said slowly. "But how do I do that? You know how long I've been hearing that shit."

Paige was about to answer when the waitress came up. "Sorry for the delay ladies, seems that there are folks who don't have solid work ethics any longer."

"What do you mean?" Tinsleigh asked.

"Two of our waitresses called out this morning, leaving me holding the bag."

"Oh my goodness, you poor thing!"

"The joke's on them, though, because Esther is tired of their crap and plans to fire them if they show up tomorrow. I just have to hold on until lunch."

"You can do it," Paige said encouragingly. "No one seems like they're stressed so you're obviously making it happen."

"It helps that so many are regulars of mine. I can almost tell you what they are in the mood for when they walk in the door. So, what would you ladies like today?"

"How about we place our drink and food orders now to help you out?" Tinsleigh asked.

"That would help, absolutely, but only if you're ready."

"I would like scrambled eggs, buttered toast, and a fruit plate," Tinsleigh replied. "And can I have a glass of orange juice and one of ice water?"

The waitress jotted her order down and looked at Paige, asking, "What about you?"

"Let's make that two," Paige replied. "Plus, I'd like a coffee."

"Got it," the waitress said. "Be back in a few with your drinks."

"Jonathan, I need you to *want* this," Thorne said, an edge of frustration in his voice.

"Man, it's not as easy as I thought it would be," the other man said, "I mean, dieting has never been my thing."

"Ah, I think I've figured out the problem," Thorne replied.

"How so?"

"It's not a diet, it's a *lifestyle* change. Do you think I forego my beer or wings on game day?"

"Well, no, but…"

"There are no 'buts' here, Jonathan. I have worked the foods I enjoy into my eating plan, plain and simple. You like wings and the occasional beer? Then figure out what you can eat and work it into that day's plan. Are you doing the meal prep?"

"Not exactly."

"Okay, what the hell does that mean, not exactly?"

The younger man looked at him and said, "It means no, I haven't. I just don't know where to start, to be honest. I mean, I've been living on Ramen and microwave meals for so long, I have no clue."

Making a decision, he said, "Go get showered and changed, I'm going to help you, so you know how easy this can honestly be, okay?"

He saw the relief cross Jonathan's face and knew he had made a good call. "Thanks, man. I want this to succeed. Hell, when I was in school, I was in phenomenal shape."

"Don't thank me yet, we still have to shop and shit," Thorne replied. "Now hurry up.

I'm going to take care of a few things in the office so come grab me when you're ready to roll out."

"Oh, Tiny, I love that one," Paige said as she came out of the dressing room. "Turn around so I can see the back."

She slowly turned, liking how the dress swished below her knees. It was a deep maroon with a modest V-neck, three-quarter sleeves that were flowy and had a touch of lace, and a cinched-in waist that seemed to flatter her figure. "He's going to love how you look in that," Paige told her as she stood and walked all the way around. "Oh yeah, this dress is it!"

"We've got heels that match," the salesgirl said, coming up to them. "Would you like to try a pair on?"

"Sure," Tinsleigh replied, looking at herself in the mirror. Shining eyes, tousled curls that hung nearly to her waist. *Her waist! Dang, working out was paying off.*

The salesgirl came back with a pair of heels and she slipped them on. "What do you think, Paige?"

"Oh, Tiny," Paige whispered. "You look like the sugar plum fairy right now!"

"Yeah, right, whatever."

"That. That right there – you need to stop making statements that put yourself down," Paige stated.

"She's right," the salesgirl said. "You look absolutely stunning. I wish I had your figure. Most men like a woman with a few curves."

"Well up until about two months ago, my curves were more plentiful," Tinsleigh admitted. "Then I found this awesome personal trainer and now? They're still there but toned."

"You look fantastic. What's the event?" the salesgirl asked.

"She's meeting her boyfriend's family at his sister's wedding," Paige replied, shooing Tinsleigh back toward the dressing room to get changed.

"He's going to love that dress."

"Honestly? He seems to like whatever she wears," Paige admitted. "But she has a hard time believing in herself."

"Why?"

"Because I was never good enough for my mother or my ex," Tinsleigh replied, coming back out from the dressing room with the dress and shoes. "I'm finding out they were full of shit."

"Uh, yeah they were," the salesgirl said, taking the items from her hands. "Did you need anything else?"

"No, I've got the undergarments that will work for this I think."

"Great. Let's get you checked out," the salesgirl replied.

Once she was done checking out, she said, "Thanks for all your help today. I'm probably more nervous than I need to be about this, but it's important to him, so it's important to me, you know?"

The salesgirl nodded, handing her the garment bag with the dress in it, along with the shoe bag. "I hope you have a great time."

"You mean I can grill most of my meats?" Jonathan asked.

"Absolutely. Get one of those indoor grill things for the winter. My girlfriend buys her meats in larger packages then breaks them down and freezes them, which is a great way to do it and it's cost-efficient. Then, she spends Sundays preparing side dishes that will keep and putting them in the fridge so all she has to do is decide which meat she wants and pull it out either the day before if she has to marinade it or that morning. And trust me, she loved the microwave life for its convenience," he told the other man.

"I can do that," Jonathan said. "Most Sundays, I go to church with my grams then come home and watch whatever game is on."

"Sounds like you've got a plan, then. Now, I want to talk to you about adding a few more things."

The ringing of her phone had her smiling when she saw who was calling. "Hey, you!" she said, a smile on her face.

"Hey, sweetheart. Just checking to see how your morning is going. You're not overdoing it, are you?"

"No, as a matter of fact, Paige is driving us back now."

"Did you find what you were looking for?"

"I did, it's really pretty."

"She looks like the sugar plum fairy!" Paige yelled.

Thorne laughed when he heard Paige's voice. "I can't wait to see you in it, Tinsleigh," he said. "I'll be over after I'm done here, you enjoy lunch with your dad, okay?"

"See you when you get there, Thorne."

"Be sure to nap some."

She rolled her eyes, causing Paige to laugh, and said, "I'm much better."

"I know, but you still need your rest."

Chapter Nine

Three weeks later

She smiled as she packed the last of her things. They'd be leaving after Thorne was done at the gym for the day and head up to his dad and step-mom's house for the wedding. The past three weeks had been busy, even though the first week, she had spent more time 'taking it easy' than anything. *At least you're caught up on stuff for your clients, Tins.* Still, even though she was caught up, she went ahead and got her laptop and packed it up just to be on the safe side. Feeling a nudge at her ankle, she looked down and smiled. "C'mon, Widget, let's go outside, boy."

The little brown dog trotted alongside, his tail wagging. All three animals had settled into the house as if they had always been there, and she had sent pictures to the woman she had adopted them through to show how well they were doing. Once outside, she tossed the ball for a bit until he came back and collapsed by her legs, panting. "You know, Widget, you've gotta be in good shape around here to keep up with me," she teased, crouching and giving him a belly rub. "Now, let's go make sure y'all don't need anything while I'm gone, okay? Paige is gonna be here to take care of you guys."

Now that the bags were packed, it was time to make sure the room Paige would be using was fresh. It was something her grammy had ingrained in her, to always have the guest rooms ready for company. With Thorne using one of the rooms, she had to double-check the other. Since her surgery, he had stayed every night, even though she told him it wasn't necessary. After the first few days, he had given her a modified workout program, and she had finally met his new client, Jonathan.

Grabbing a clean set of sheets, she started making the bed and thought about Jonathan. And Paige. The two of them were like oil and water and yet...she could see that they were attracted to one another. *I bet Paige is acting like she is to encourage him. She gives him* hell *whenever we're at the gym!* Must be working though, because he had stopped bitching about how hard things were and had started buckling down. Once the bed was made, she got fresh towels and put them in the bathroom, imagining Paige rolling her eyes at how old-fashioned she was sometimes. Satisfied that the room was set for Paige, she went back out and found her phone.

Tinsleigh: Hey, do we need to bring any stuff to do food prep?

Thorne: No, Dad and Sienna eat pretty clean, so we'll be okay. What are you doing?

Tinsleigh: Just finished packing and getting Paige's room ready for her.

Thorne: And you did that after working out this morning?

Tinsleigh: Um, yeah.

Thorne: Aren't you still supposed to be taking it easy?

Tinsleigh: Got the all-clear from the doctor yesterday, remember? I had to bring you the note so I could bump my workouts up.

Thorne: And it's going to be a busy few days. Please, ease this old man's mind and go relax with the pets!
Tinsleigh: You're not old, Thorne.
Thorne: Older than you.
Tinsleigh: And?
Thorne: That means you need to respect your elders.
Tinsleigh: LOL…fine, I'll go lay down. Wake me up when you're ready to go?
Thorne: Yes.

Laughing at how silly he was being, she went in and grabbed a quick shower, braiding her hair before she put on a pair of leggings and a t-shirt. *Everything's getting too loose!* Smiling, because it meant that the eating plan and working out were doing what she wanted, she called out to the animals and grinned when they all came running into the bedroom. "C'mon, guys, Thorne says I have to nap."

He walked into the house and noticed how quiet it was. Smiling because it looked like she had listened, he went into the room he had been using and quickly packed his bag for the trip. Bringing it back out to the front door, he went to the master bedroom and saw hers sitting there, so he grabbed them as well. Once back in the room, he saw her curled up sleeping, the three animals cuddled all around. *Damn, I hate to wake her up.* Looking at his watch, he saw they still had some time before they had to leave, so he slipped off his shoes and grabbed a throw before crawling into the bed and pulling her into his arms.

"Hey, sleepyhead, we need to get going."

She heard his voice next to her ear and felt his warm arm heavy around her waist and smiled. "I'm feeling nice and cozy, though."

"Yeah, me too, but we've got a few hours of driving to get through, sweetheart. I've got everything ready to go out to the truck, so if you want to get Widget fed, we'll be ready to go in a few."

Sitting up, she stretched and then stood up, heading into the bathroom. "Paige was going to feed Widget, so give me a few and I'll be ready."

"I'll get the truck started. The temperature has dropped a little bit," he called out as he walked out of the bedroom. "C'mon, Widget, let's go out, little man." The little brown dog wagged his tail and followed him to the front door where he grabbed their bags and then headed out to the truck. Once the dog was done, he called him back in and went into the kitchen to grab a couple of waters and make sure the cats had dry food.

"You ready?" she asked, coming down the hallway, jacket over her arm and purse on her shoulder.

"I am, yes. You don't want to put that on?" he asked, motioning to the jacket.

"No, I don't like wearing them when I'm in a vehicle."

"It should be warm enough. You're sure Paige is feeding Widget?"

"Positive. She just texted."

"Then let's get this show on the road."

They hit a freak snowstorm which delayed their arrival by an hour and by the time he pulled into his dad's driveway, she was dozing. Putting the car in park and shutting it off, he got out and grabbing her jacket, went to the passenger side. "C'mon, sweetheart, you're going to want your jacket," he said, gently shaking her awake. "It's a lot colder than we anticipated."

She felt the cool night air and shivered. "I'll be glad to get inside," she replied, putting her jacket on and getting down.

"You and me both. You ready?" he asked, his arms full of their bags.

"I can carry something, Thorne."

"Not on my watch. You can get the door."

They headed up to the front door and it opened just as they reached it, a booming voice saying, "Give me some of those, and let's get this pretty lady inside."

"Hey, Dad. This is Tinsleigh Martin. Tinsleigh, this is my dad, Tom Baker, and my step-mom, Sienna."

"It's a pleasure to meet you both," Tinsleigh said, holding her hand out.

"Likewise, pretty lady, now let's get inside and out of this chill air."

Once inside, Thorne said, "Sorry we're so late, weather got bad about halfway here."

"No worries, did you eat?" Sienna asked.

"We did."

"Well, you know where your room is," Tom stated. "We're going to head on up now that y'all have made it safe and sound. Glad you're here, Son. See you both in the morning."

"Good night, Dad, Sienna. See y'all in the morning."

Tinsleigh's wide eyes met his and he grinned. "What's the matter?" he asked, leaning close.

"Are...are we *sharing* a room?"

"Yep," he replied, walking through the foyer and down a hallway to another door. Opening it, he motioned for her to go on up the stairs, turning the lights on so she could see the steps. He put the suitcases on the steps and closed and locked the door behind him, before picking their bags up once again and following her.

"This is your room?" she asked, looking around.

"Yeah, when Dad and Sienna married, I was a senior in high school. They wanted me to have my own space since I was about to head off to college, so they took the room over the garage and made it into my room. Even though I've been out on my own for years, Sienna insists on keeping it for me for my visits."

"Thorne, this is almost big enough to be an apartment," she said, looking to the area that was set up with a couch and a fireplace and a television.

"Let me give you the fifty-cent tour," he replied, holding out his hand. When she took it, he walked her over to a set of doors, saying, "This is the bathroom," as he opened the door. She saw a huge claw-foot tub, a separate enclosed shower, and a double vanity sink. A partially opened door within the bathroom was where the toilet was tucked away.

"Mighty fancy digs for a guy in high school," she teased as he walked her over to another set of doors.

"Yeah, I was popular, all right. I can access the room through the house or through the garage. Made it handy when I was in college, that's for sure."

"Oh, I bet."

"Here's the closet if you want to hang your dress up." He wisely left her last comment alone. *Do I tell her now that I replaced the bed when I split with Marisa? Naw, now's not the time.*

"I'm going to run back down and grab us something to drink. Why don't you get changed for bed? I'm sure Gloria will want to meet you bright and early."

She pulled her dress out and hung it before replying, "Okay. And you're sure your brother is at your mother's?"

"That's what Gloria said, yes."

"Good. I am too tired for my filter to be in place."

He started laughing and said, "I'll be right back."

She grabbed her pajamas and toiletries bag and headed into the bathroom. By the time he came back up with some waters, she was standing by the bed. "I...I wasn't sure what side you would want," she murmured, looking at everything but him.

"Sleep on your normal side, sweetheart. I'm sleeping on top of the covers," he replied.

Climbing into bed, she sat against the headboard and took the water he gave her, opening it and drinking half the bottle. "Thanks for this," she said as he sat on the other side of the bed, motioning to the water.

"You know we're gonna get up and go for a run, right?"

"I've got my stuff, seems my personal trainer would be upset if I wasn't working out while out of town."

"I've heard he can be a hard ass."

She burst into laughter at the look he had on his face – all stern with no smile. "Yeah, he's a tough one, that's for sure, but I'm sure when my date sees me in my dress, he'll agree it's been worth it."

Turning toward her, he cupped her chin and said, "You've always been worth it, Tinsleigh. Always. Now, get settled so we can get some sleep."

Curling up on her side away from him, she smiled when he settled down and put his arm around her waist, pulling the throw from the end of the bed over her exposed arm. "Good night, Thorne."

"Night, sweetheart. Sleep well."

He woke up a few hours later and lay there, listening to her breathe. The light floral scent she wore enveloped him and made him want things he had long given up on. When his stomach grumbled, he eased himself away, figuring that some scrambled eggs would be enough to hold him until the next morning. Gently kissing her temple, he whispered, "Soon."

Down in the kitchen, he grabbed the carton of eggs and a bowl. He was in the process of cracking the eggs, lost in thoughts of Tinsleigh and where they were as a couple when the cloying scent of White Diamonds drifted into the room. *Marisa.* Internally steeling himself, he turned and saw her standing in the kitchen wearing a peignoir set that was more appropriate for the bedroom, not roaming the kitchen in the middle of the night. "What are you doing here, Marisa?" he asked, crossing his arms over his chest. "Y'all were supposed to be at Mom's house, not here."

"We had a last-minute change of plans," she replied, coming closer and reaching out as if to touch him.

"Don't," he stated. "You lost that right years ago."

"Thorne, why do you have to be like this? It's been *years* and you still won't talk to either one of us."

"And until now, I was content to keep it that way, to be honest. How the fuck am I supposed to feel when I come home from a trip to find my *brother* fucking my fiancée over the back of the couch?"

"I...it..."

"Just stop. There's nothing either of you can say that will make it right. If you had wanted him, you should have done the decent thing and broken it off with me. I wouldn't have been happy, but it would have been the right thing to do, you know? But no, you two started something while I was gone, then you compounded it by running off to Vegas and getting married."

"But we...you and I were always good together, Thorne."

"Again, that ended several years ago, Marisa. And I have no intention of going back."

"It's not like you're seeing anyone."

She woke up and realized he wasn't in bed any longer. Getting up, she went to the restroom and then went in search of him, her stomach leading the way. Hearing voices coming from the kitchen, she stopped just out of eyesight and listened, her heart in her throat hearing Marisa's last comment. *Thorne wouldn't do that to you, he's not Denny.* Still, that little voice in her head was scared about what he would say.

"As a matter of fact, Marisa, I *am* seeing someone. A wonderful woman who you couldn't even hold a candle to, if I'm being wholly truthful. So perhaps I should say thank you, because if you hadn't cheated, I never would have met her and found the woman I want to spend the rest of my life with."

Her heart melted at his words. *It's time to claim your man, Tinsleigh. He's shown you he's nothing like Denny and your heart and body will be safe in his hands.*

Walking into the kitchen, she headed straight to him uncaring that her braid had started coming out and she was in a camisole and sleep pants. "Hey, I missed you," she murmured as she encircled his waist. "You forgot to kiss me before you came downstairs."

He grinned down at her and pulled her closer, knowing she could feel how her nearness affected him. "Came down to make us some eggs, sweetheart," he replied, leaning his forehead against hers. "Let me introduce you, yeah?"

"If you must," she whispered, a grin playing on her lips.

Turning in his arms, she clasped his hands that were at her waist and pasted a smile on her face. "Tinsleigh, this is Marisa, my brother's wife."

"Hello. You must have thought your husband was down here, dressed like that," Tinsleigh said. She felt Thorne's chuckle even as Marisa's face darkened.

"Well, I never..." Marisa stammered.

"It appears that you were trying to, but I'll give you a heads up, Thorne's off the market."

"How dare you?" Marissa screeched.

"I dare because I *heard* you propositioning him. Shame on you! Does your husband know you're like this? Oh wait, never mind, he *does* seeing as you cheated with him. Now go away, you're not wanted," she stated, turning her back on the woman.

Hearing the stamping feet as they fled the kitchen, she buried her face in his t-shirt and said, "Sorry, but apparently I left my filter somewhere between home and here."

He lifted her chin and she could see the grin on his face. "Sweetheart, I've never had anyone do that for me. To say it was hotter than hell is an understatement. Now, you mentioned something about a kiss?"

Blushing, she raised her hands and looped them around his neck. "Yeah, about that, I kind of figured it was time, am I too late?"

"Never," he whispered before claiming her lips in his.

Holy shit! Soft yet firm, his lips took over, molding against hers and causing her body to curl further into his. Moaning slightly, she felt his tongue glide across and she opened, letting him in and meeting him more than halfway. He lightly nipped her bottom lip then stroked his tongue over it. She flicked hers against his and felt the rumble of his groan go through her.

Long, breathless minutes passed before they broke apart, panting slightly as they stood there, forehead to forehead.

"Wow…what…what was that?" she finally asked once she could breathe again and the stars behind her eyes had stopped flashing.

"Our last first kiss," he murmured. "You're mine and I'm yours, Tinsleigh. Until we draw our last breaths."

"I like the sound of that, Thorne."

"Me, too, sweetheart. Me too. Now, how about I make us some scrambled eggs to tide us over until breakfast?"

"Sounds good, what do you want me to do?"

"Well, for starters, I think we need to pull away from one another."

"But I don't want to!"

He chuckled at her faux pout before placing a kiss on her lips. "The sooner we get them done, the sooner we can go back upstairs."

"I approve of this plan," she said, stepping away and going to the fridge. "Want some juice?"

"Yeah, we're going to be running so I want to make sure we're ready."

They worked in companionable silence with light touches and kisses every time they were within each other's space. She had just gotten the plates down when she heard a male voice say, "What in the hell did you do to my wife?"

Turning around, she saw a man who could only be Thorne's brother. Thorne was taller and bulkier, but they shared the same hair and eye color. "I didn't *do* anything to your wife," Thorne replied, taking the pan and scooping out the eggs onto the proffered plates.

"Then why is she upstairs crying?"

"Probably because she propositioned him and was turned down," Tinsleigh stated.

"Who the hell are you?" Roger asked, turning toward her.

"I'm his, and I didn't appreciate *your wife* coming down here dressed for a bedroom romp trying to put her claws into him. The two of you are a piece of work and from what I can tell, deserve one another."

"How dare you?"

"Excuse me? I don't think so, buddy. Go ask *your wife* what she said to Thorne. I'm sure you'll get something totally different, but I *heard* her. I also heard him tell her to back off. Several times. So, you may want to tend to your own yard before you come down here and get into his."

"So, you've got a woman speaking for you now, Thorne?"

"She was the one who said something to Marisa that had her leaving. I happen to agree with her, so why repeat it? Now, seems you have something to take care of and so do we."

With that, Thorne took the plates and silverware and led Tinsleigh out of the kitchen, leaving Roger standing there with a confused look on his face.

Back upstairs, the door locked against anyone, he led her to the sitting area and handed her a plate. Seeing the look on her face, he said, "What's the matter?"

"Did…did I go too far? I mean, she was your ex and he is your brother. I just couldn't…there was no way I was letting him think that *you* did something when it was all her."

"No, you didn't 'go too far', Tinsleigh. They've both needed that for years and I wasn't in the place or headspace to do it. Of course, I never expected that she would ever try something like that on me."

"Why not? You're a good man, Thorne Baker. Thoughtful, caring, hardworking. The outside package doesn't hurt either!"

He started laughing as he put his plate down and pulled her close. "C'mon, pretty girl, let's curl up and neck like teenagers."

"I like the way you think."

Chapter Ten

"Y'know, I never did this," she confessed as they laid curled, face-to-face, on the couch in the sitting area.

"Did what? Make out?"

"Yeah. It wasn't 'proper' or 'seemly' for a girl of my station to 'act like her hormones ruled her' so I may not be very good."

"I'm sure you'll be fine, sweetheart. Besides, we're in this for the long haul, so we'll be figuring it out together. We've just gotta keep our lines of communication open is all."

"I can do that," she whispered, her hand playing with the hem of his shirt. "Have I ever told you that when you don't have a shirt on my mouth goes completely dry?"

"Why?"

"Not sure if it's the muscles, the chest hair that my fingers want to play with, or the fact that your abs are totally lickable."

He burst into laughter at her words. "Lickable?" he finally got out through his chuckles.

"Yeah," she whispered, leaning in and nuzzling his neck.

"Hmmm, so since you've never had a proper making out, I guess we won't be hitting all the bases," he said, lightly stroking her back.

"We'll see," she said, her voice a husky murmur as she leaned up and captured his lips.

For long minutes, they lost themselves in one another. He figured out that the spot behind her ear had her arching toward him, and she realized that being pressed against him was the best thing she'd ever felt. As his lips moved down her neck, she moved restlessly, wanting his hands and mouth to keep going.

"You okay?" he murmured against her throat.

"Mmmhmm," she breathed out.

He quickly realized that his body was reacting like a teenager and he pulled slightly back. "You're making me feel like I'm sixteen again."

"I don't think I was ever sixteen," she said, pulling at his shirt.

"Minx."

"Ah, but I'm *your* minx now," she replied.

"This is true." Standing up, he scooped her into his arms and moved toward the bed. "But, I'm not sixteen and need more room to move around."

She looked at him and pulled her camisole over her head. "Your turn," she stated.

"You're killing me, woman," he murmured, pulling his t-shirt off. Now face-to-face on the bed, he stroked her cheek and leaned in to say, "I'm falling in love with you, Tinsleigh. Never thought it would happen again, but you've captured my heart and soul."

Sparkling eyes met his and she replied, "I'm glad to hear that, Thorne, because I already love you."

I've died and gone to heaven. Each stroke of his hand, every brush of his lips had her wanting things she never thought would be possible. Sex with Denny had been…okay…but if she was honest, he had never set her on fire the way she was right now. "Thorne?" she asked, her voice little more than a whisper.

"What, sweetheart?" he replied, raising his head to look at her.

"I want more. I want you. Here. Now."

"Are you sure? We can wait until we get home."

"Yes, I'm sure and no, I don't want to wait."

He sat up and looked down at her, seeing the rosy cheeks and kiss-swollen lips. Leaning over, he helped her sit up and then, took her braid down so her curls flowed down her back. "I've dreamed of your hair surrounding me," he murmured, as he then gently placed her back down and lowered himself so he was half on and half off her body. The feel of her hardened nipples against his chest had him groaning as he took her lips in his once again.

Even as the storm raged outside, the room grew warmer, with soft whispers and murmurs tracing a path along them both. As his hand stroked along her hip, she writhed before reaching down to take her pajama bottoms off. "There's no hurry, sweetheart," he whispered, even as his hands helped her and then removed his own so they were finally skin on skin.

"I know, but they were getting in the way."

Once again, he leaned back so he was looking down at her. "You're so fucking beautiful," he replied, seeing how her full breasts were plumped up, the nipples hard and ready for his lips and mouth. "And these right here," he said, lightly gripping her hips, "have given me many thoughts since I first met you."

"Oh yeah?"

"God, yes," he stated, leaning down and lightly nipping the skin where his thumb was, which caused her to writhe. "No clue what kind of experience you've had, Tinsleigh, and honestly don't care, because we're making our own memories."

"As long as we have fun and love one another at the end of the day, I'm game for just about anything," she said. She somehow knew that sex with him was going to be earth-changing.

"Oh, I can guarantee we'll have fun," he said, a grin spreading across his face.

Once again, he worked to stoke the fire inside her, sure that he wouldn't last long once he was buried inside. Stroking her body, lightly teasing places where she moaned, he finally leaned in and took a nipple in his mouth.

"Oh my God," she hissed out between clenched teeth as his lips, teeth and tongue made her move restlessly.

Moving to the other side, he gave that nipple the same attention, keeping his hand moving toward the warmth he could feel against his hip. Reaching the apex of her thighs, he gently stroked across her mound and grinned when her legs parted. The essence of her surrounding him, her perfume, the body wash she used, and the unmistakable wetness that his fingers touched had him groaning out loud. *She's going to be the death of me.*

He heard her breath hitch when his thumb hit her clit and he began a slow, circular motion, keeping the pressure heavy enough that she began to pant. "Thorne?"

"Hmm?" he replied, his mouth now kissing across her stomach and moving further down.

"Feels good," she murmured, one of her hands clutching the sheets while the other stroked him wherever she could reach.

"Gonna feel better," he replied, reaching what he was sure was nirvana. A slow swipe of his tongue had her arching her back and soon, there were no words spoken as he gripped her hips and stroked her body to a height she had never before experienced.

"Thorne!" she cried out, her orgasm hitting the second he put one finger inside her heat. He continued to pump in and out, while he sucked on her clit until she began to pull away. Moving back up her body, he took her lips in a punishing kiss and mimicked with his tongue what he would soon be doing with his body.

Lining himself up against her swollen pussy lips, he felt her hand reach down and grip him. "May not last long," he warned.

"I don't care, I just want *you*," she breathed out on a sigh, her eyes never leaving his.

Slowly, oh-so-slowly, he entered her and they both sighed when he was fully buried within her warm, wet heat. "You feel so good, sweetheart," he said against her lips.

Looping her arms around his neck, she kissed him before saying, "Love me, Thorne. Make me yours."

For what felt like days but was probably only minutes if he was honest, he moved within her, going deeper when she wrapped her legs around his low back. When she moaned, he said, "Like that?"

"God, yes," she moaned. "Please don't stop."

"I couldn't even if I wanted to," he replied, his pace quickening. He could feel the familiar tingles racing up his spine. "Tinsleigh, we didn't use a condom, do you want me to pull out?"

"I want you. I'm good, I take birth control for…um…other issues. And after…"

"Don't. Their names have no place in our bed. I was too," he stated.

"Then, like I said before, make me yours."

Reaching between him, he began stroking her clit again and when he felt her pussy start contracting, he thrust a few more times before he emptied himself in her.

When he felt he would collapse, he gathered her in his arms, still connected and fell to his side so they were face-to-face once again. "That was awesome," she finally said. He looked at her and saw her shining eyes now sated and felt how relaxed she was against him.

"Yeah, sweetheart. Let me get you cleaned up, okay?"

Clean up with Thorne was fun she mused, curled against him with his front to her back. It had involved a quick shower and another mind-blowing orgasm before he carried her back to bed. "Love you, Tinsleigh," he whispered, kissing her behind the ear.

"Mmm, love you too, Thorne."

"C'mon, sleepy girl, we've got to get our run in before we do all the family things that Gloria planned today."

"Can't we just stay in bed?" she murmured, pulling the covers over her head.

"As much as I want to say yes, I don't want my dad or stepmom looking for us."

The covers flew back, and he saw her face light up in a blush before she said, "Oh my

God, they're going to *know* what we did this morning!"

He chuckled as he leaned down and kissed her. "Sweetheart, they put us in the same room. Thinking they figured we were already doing it." When wide eyes looked his way, he laughed harder and said, "C'mon, beautiful, let's get our run out of the way."

She made quick work of her morning routine and dressed in the shorts and t-shirt she brought to run in. When he saw her, he said, "You may want your tights, it's pretty chilly."

"Really?"

"Yeah, go ahead and get them on. I don't want you getting sick."

Grabbing her tights, she took off her shorts and quickly put them on, not missing the look in his eyes. "Uh-uh, you said we couldn't stay in bed," she said when he moved closer.

"Yeah, but you need a kiss," he murmured, taking her lips in his.

———

Down in the kitchen, he grabbed a couple of waters and they were headed out the front door before anyone else saw them. If his luck held, they could get their workout in and be back, showered, and downstairs before breakfast. At least, that was his plan.

"So where are we running?" she asked as they stretched.

"A trail that's not far from here," he replied, helping her up. "You ready?"

"Yup. Don't want my personal trainer disappointed in me."

"Not gonna happen, sweetheart."

He kept their pace steady. At this point, it was more about building stamina and endurance for the triathlon she would be participating in after the new year. He had signed her and Paige up, and was going to see if Jonathan wanted to get involved as well. Glancing at her, he saw her take a drink of water and grinned. She was so beautiful, even all sweaty, and he was thrilled to see how her backbone had showed up earlier in the day. "Okay, we turn around here," he said as they reached the reservoir. It was one of his favorite runs, the countryside peaceful enough that he could think and let the stress of life go.

"I like this run," she said, turning around. "Very peaceful."

"You're doing great, Tinsleigh."

"Thanks to my kick-ass personal trainer."

"That is just a small part, sweetheart. *You're* the one doing the hard work, I'm just giving you the tools."

"So, what are we going to do today?"

"Gloria wants us to go to this place that has a 'sky hike' with ropes, and a rock wall, and a zip line."

"Those all sound like fun, even though I'm not sure I can do the zip line," she admitted.

"Why not?"

"They've got weight limits."

He looked at her and was about to say something when he remembered that she didn't know where she was at right now. "Tinsleigh? Trust me when I say you're well within the limits to do the zip line if you want to."

"I am?"

"Yup. Remember, I've been doing the measurements and weight. You were under it to begin with and now? Yeah."

She smiled before saying, "I'm glad. I like being more active and I know, being with you, that'll be a lifelong thing."

"Absolutely," he replied, slowing up as they reached the house. "C'mon, we can stretch in the living room, it's a bit chilly out still."

"Works for me. Although I'm definitely going to need a shower. Again."

"I was counting on it," he whispered as they walked into the house.

"Ah, glad you guys are back!" Sienna said. "Breakfast will be ready in about thirty minutes or so."

"We've got to stretch and take a quick shower, but don't hold it on account of us," Thorne replied, taking her hand and moving into the family room.

"Nonsense. Your sister wants to go over today's itinerary," Sienna said, laughing at the expression he made. "Oh, and just so you know, your dad made them leave when he got up and realized they had come here. I understand there was a problem earlier today and I'm so sorry for that."

"Sienna, it's not your fault or Dad's. They made the choice to come here and had to hear a few things they likely didn't want to hear but at least it was here and not at G's wedding or reception."

"You're right, but this house has always been your safe haven, Thorne."

"Still is, Sienna," he replied.

"I'll leave y'all to it then. Oh, and your dad said if there was um…anything you were looking for, check the cupboard underneath the bathroom sink."

He looked at his stepmom and saw her blush and realized what she meant. "We're good, Sienna."

Once she left the room, Tinsleigh said, "What did she mean?"

"Condoms, sweetheart. My dad made sure there were condoms in the bathroom."

"Oh, my God, no he didn't! I can't face him!" she exclaimed, her face turning bright red.

"Sure you can. C'mon, up now, we have a quick shower to take and breakfast to eat."

"Mmmm, I kinda like your idea of a 'quick shower'," she murmured as he powered into her from behind.

"Well, I didn't think I could wait until later, sweetheart, not after having seen you running in that outfit," he grunted out, his hand going down to her mound to stroke her clit.

"Shorts? A t-shirt?" she asked, swiveling her hips then grinning when she heard his moan. *No clue who this sex diva is but I kinda like her.* Sex with Denny was almost by the book. A few perfunctory kisses, maybe a grope or two and then he would plow away, uncaring or perhaps unknowing that her body wasn't always ready. Sex with Thorne? While she only had a few times to compare it to, it was light years away from what she had experienced before and she fucking loved it.

"Sweetheart, *anything* you wear has me thinking of you like this," he muttered before saying, "now come for me, Tinsleigh."

Could have been his words, could have been how deliciously he was pounding her, could have been his thumb putting just the right amount of pressure on her clit, but she detonated, her moans mingling with his as he finished at the same time.

After what felt like days, he straightened, pulling out of her and causing her to moan, before he turned her under the shower spray. "Let's get cleaned up."

"Ah, there the lovebirds are," Tom said, earning a swat from his wife.

"Tom! You're making the poor girl blush, knock it off!"

"Hey now, I'm just happy my boy's happy," he replied, stealing a piece of bacon from the plate she was carrying to the table.

"Sorry about..." Tom started.

"No worries, Dad. I already told Sienna it was better it happened here than at Gloria's wedding or reception. This way, they know to stay the fuck away from us."

"Let me help you, Sienna," Tinsleigh said, going over to the counter and grabbing a platter piled high with scrambled eggs.

"Oh, honey, you don't have to do that."

"Don't mind helping."

"So, where's the bride-to-be?" Thorne asked.

"I'm *here!*" Gloria screamed as she launched herself at her brother. Catching her in mid-air, he swung her around before putting her down and kissing her head.

"It's about time, we were going to waste away," he teased, pulling one of her curls.

"Tinsleigh? This is my baby sister, Gloria. Gloria, this is Tinsleigh."

"I'm so happy to meet you finally!" Gloria enthused, going over and hugging Tinsleigh.

"Same here. Is there anything you need help with to wrap stuff up?"

"Hmm, maybe you can help me, Sienna, and Mom put the favors together later?"

"Sure, would be happy to help. So, Thorne mentioned we're going someplace where we can zip line?"

"I think I've created a monster," he said, grinning as she landed where he was standing.

"How so?" she asked as she undid the harness.

"Because this is the what, fifth time you've gone down the line?" he replied, taking her hand in his.

"I had no idea it would be so freeing!"

"I gathered that, sweetheart. We're gonna go grab something to eat before we continue on with the next thing G wants to do."

"Works for me, I'm getting hungry again."

"We're actually working out right now," he whispered in her ear.

"And we worked out in the shower, and we're gonna work out again tonight. At least I hope we are," she replied back, kissing him quickly.

"Count on it."

"Go away, Thorne, I wanna tell Tinsleigh *all* of your secrets," Gloria said as she shooed him out of the craft room where the women were gathering. He eyed the pitchers of sangria she had brought up and grinned.

"G, just remember that street runs both ways and I'm downstairs with Travis," he replied, grinning at her as he headed toward the door.

"You wouldn't dare!" she screeched.

"Maybe so…maybe no…but if you behave, I'll keep those secrets."

"Ugh, you're being a pain in my ass right now."

His laughter followed him out the door and Tinsleigh looked at his sister and winked.

"You can still tell me on the down-low," she murmured.

"So, how did you meet?" his mother, Mary, asked, as she pulled out tiny bags they were filling with almond candies.

"He was recommended to me by my doctor as a nutritionist and personal trainer," Tinsleigh replied, grabbing a bag of the candies and a stack of the bags. "Do you want the bows to be fancy or just tied?"

"Hmm, I think just tied, people like eating these so they're going to want to get into them, y'know?" Gloria replied, taking her own stack and sitting down.

"Honey, you don't look like you needed a personal trainer," Sienna stated, grabbing her stack and starting the filling process.

"Ah, but I did," Tinsleigh said, tying the first bag and moving to the next. She had decided to fill a bunch, then tie them off, then fill more. "I went through a bad divorce and gained some weight while I processed my feelings. I had started taking it off, but it wasn't fast enough. I had some kidney stones developing and my doctor recommended Thorne hoping that they would break up and pass. I started working out that week with my best friend, Paige."

"Well, you look fantastic," Mary stated. "And I can see you make my son very happy."

"He makes me happy as well."

"Did they?" Gloria asked.

"Did they what?"

"Did the kidney stones pass?"

"Um, not without surgical intervention. That's when he told me he wanted us to date."

Gloria sighed and said, "How romantic. I bet he hasn't let you out of his sight, has he?"

"Nope. He's been staying in my spare room since I came home from the hospital."

She smiled thinking about earlier in the day when they reached the top of the rope climbing thingy and he grabbed her around the waist and took a selfie, saying, "You look beautiful, all sun-kissed and windblown."

"So, you really put someone in her place this morning," G said.

"Yeah, about that...I'm sorry if I overstepped in your house, Sienna, but I couldn't stand there and listen to the lies that were being spewed by his brother, not after I heard what she said and asked him."

"Honey, you took up for your man and there's nothing wrong with that in my book, ever," Sienna replied. "I like that system you've got going, you've got a lot more done than me."

The other women looked at her stack of completed favor bags and started laughing. She was nearly done and they each only had a handful completed. "Why don't y'all fill them and I'll tie them off," she suggested.

"That works for me, my bows look like shit," G said as she started filling the bags.

"What else do you have?"

"Ugh, I have to start writing thank you notes for the shower gifts and make the bows for the pews."

"If you have the address list, I can make a label sheet for you so all you have to do is write the cards."

"Damn, I knew I liked you! Do you have a position available for best friend?"

"Already filled, but you're welcome to come along with us if you want."

Gloria started laughing. "I think I'll have a sister-in-law I actually *like* before too long."

"So, you getting nervous?" Thorne asked Travis as he grabbed them a couple of beers and the tray of wings.

"No, not really. I mean, it's a big step and we both know it, but I love your sister to death and think we're good together, y'know?"

"Yeah, I know."

"Tell me about Tinsleigh, Gloria has been going on and on about her."

"She came into the gym looking for a nutritionist and personal trainer and I knew the minute I saw her, I wanted to get to know her better."

"Are you kidding? She doesn't need a personal trainer."

"Hey now, that's my livelihood you're trying to take away. Actually, she had gained some weight the prior year and had been taking it off, but she was having a few health issues and her doctor thought it would be a good idea. I've always liked how she looked."

Tom looked at his son and smiled before getting up and saying, "I'll be right back."

"What was that about?" Thorne asked Travis.

"No clue."

Once they finished the favor bags and the first pitcher of sangria, they began making the bows for the end of the pews. When Gloria saw Tinsleigh's bow, she decreed that she was making all of them before she went downstairs to get some snacks and another pitcher of sangria made. "Jeez, she keeps filling my glass and there's no telling how these bows are going to look," Tinsleigh stated, taking a drink.

"They look fine, dear," Sienna said, as she came back in with snacks. Well, snacks was definitely a relative term. There were mini-sandwiches and cookies and iced brownies. *Maybe it'll absorb some of this alcohol.*

"So, tell me about your pets," Gloria said as she sat back down with a plate piled high. When she saw the look her mother was giving her, she rolled her eyes and started eating. "Mom, everything fits."

"I know, I know, but you don't want wedding bloat."

"Whatever, tell me about them, please?"

"Well, we stopped at an adoption event and there were three animals whose owner had passed away. They were all bonded and no one wanted to adopt them all together."

"Until you," Gloria whispered.

"Until me. Now? I have Widget, Snowflake and Brownie following me around the house. I'm really enjoying their company."

"I bet. But probably not as much as you enjoy Thorne's."

Blushing, she stood up to head downstairs. "Give me a few, I'm going to go get my laptop if you'll grab that list?" With Gloria's laughter following her, she went back downstairs then over to Thorne's room.

Spotting her while coming back out of the kitchen, he pulled her close. "What're you doing, sweetheart?" he asked.

"Grabbing my laptop so I can do the address labels for Gloria, so she can work on her thank you notes."

"How's it going? Are you surviving the inquisition?"

"Ha ha, very funny. As a matter of fact, it's going very well."

Leaning in, he captured her lips, tasting the fruity sangria when his tongue started dueling with hers. "Mmm, delicious," he whispered, pulling back to look at her.

Hooded eyes gazed back at him and he smiled before saying, "Thinking I like this look on you, sweetheart."

"What look?" she asked.

"The hot and bothered one."

"Only when you're around."

Kissing her once more, he said, "I'll let you get back to the nattering hens. Hopefully, it won't be too much longer."

"I know, I just want to curl up with you and watch a movie."

"We can do that…and anything else you've got in mind."

"Guess you'll have to wait and see what that might be," she said, grinning as she moved away.

Back in the den, he handed out the beers he had grabbed and was about to sit down when his dad said, "She's the one, Thorne."

"What?"

"I said, she's the one for you."

"It's kind of early days, Dad."

"Maybe so. Anyhow, I want you to have this," he replied, taking a small box out of his pocket.

"What is it?" Thorne asked.

"It was your grandmother's engagement ring."

Thorne opened the box and saw the white-gold band surrounded by small diamonds with a larger, princess-cut one in the middle. "It's gorgeous."

"The time may not be right now, but it's coming, and I want you to have it," Tom stated.

"Thanks, Dad," he replied, slipping the box in his pocket.

Hearing noise at the door, the men turned to see the women standing there. "We're done!" Gloria exclaimed as she headed toward Travis.

"You ladies hungry?" Tom asked.

"Mmm, no, we had sandwiches and stuff upstairs. You want anything?" Sienna questioned.

"We had wings and I tossed some brats on the grill."

"I think we're all good, then. What's on the itinerary for tomorrow?"

"We're getting pampered at the spa," Gloria replied. "Oh, and Tinsleigh, you're going with us."

"I am?"

"You are, sweetheart," Thorne replied. "Gloria added you to the list when I told her I was bringing you."

"What time are we going?"

"We'll leave around eleven, grab some lunch, then spend the rest of the day getting pampered before the rehearsal dinner."

"Do we have time to work out?" Tinsleigh asked.

"If we get up early, yes. Dad's got a gym downstairs, so we'll do a quick one."

She nodded before saying, "Then I guess we better think about turning in."

"Mmmm, you've turned me into a sex fiend," she murmured as she caressed his cheek and kissed the underside of his jaw.

"How so?" he asked as his hand lightly stroked her hip.

"I had no idea it could be this much *fun*."

He burst into laughter. They had come upstairs and curled on the couch to watch a movie. Until she started stroking him. And he started kissing her. Before long, the movie was forgotten, and they were contorting themselves so he could bury himself in her.

"You've become very flexible, sweetheart, so of course, it's going to be a lot more fun."

"I think it's you."

He leaned down to nuzzle her neck before whispering, "I think it's *us*, sweetheart. Because it's never been like this with anyone. *Ever*. And that may have some wanting me to toss my man-card away, but I don't really give a rat's ass. We were made for one another, Tinsleigh."

"You really think so?"

"Sweetheart, I was attracted to you the first time we met. *All* of you," he said, as his hands stroked down her body.

"My grammy…my grammy used to say that the measure of a man who truly loved a woman was that he would love her whether she was a scrawny ninety pounds or a whopping three hundred," she whispered.

"Now you're getting it," he whispered back. "I don't give a fuck if you lose another pound. What I *do* care about is that you're happy and healthy. If working out and being fit does that for you, then I'm ecstatic. If sitting on the couch eating chocolate while you work does it? Again, I'll support you. Tinsleigh, I love you, warts and all," he said, leaning in to kiss her.

He felt the wetness as it ran down her face and pulled back. "Sweetheart? Why are you crying?"

"I...I don't know," she admitted as he wiped her face. "I...I've never had anyone in my life love me like that, except maybe Paige and her family."

"Tinsleigh, I know we're not there yet, but I hope you know where we're headed."

"And that would be?" she asked, wanting to know if what her heart was saying was true.

"You're going to wear my rings and bear our children," he whispered. "Now, let's head over to that comfortable bed so I can show you again what you mean to me."

Chapter Eleven

Heading down to the basement gym the next morning, she grinned when he swatted her ass playfully. The night before hadn't ended until just before dawn and she felt well-loved and sated. "Okay, boss-man, where do we start?"

"Treadmill, shortstuff. Twenty minutes to warm up, then we'll do some weights."

She looked around at the gym and was impressed. All of the equipment was on a smaller scale than the gym, but it was still sufficient to put in the workout she needed. "Why is this so well-equipped?" she asked as she started a slow jog.

"Heart problems run in my family and after my dad had open heart surgery, he wanted to be able to rehab himself so that he would be here for his grandkids."

"Is that when they started their lifestyle change?" she asked, bumping up the angle a bit.

"Yeah, he called me and I came out and we did the same thing that I did with you. In fact, I need to check with Gloria to see if the Gobble Jog sign-up is open yet."

"What in the hell is a Gobble Jog?"

"It's a five-K run on Thanksgiving morning. The entry fees collected go to buy turkey and the fixings for those in the community who need help."

"Are we...are we going to run in it?"

"I thought we could. I know it's not a full triathlon, but the run itself is about how long you will run during one and it'll be a great way for you to see where you're at right now."

"Okay, sign me up."

"Planned on it, shortstuff. Now, let's get these weights done so you can go get glammed up."

"What do you mean, he got me a massage?" Tinsleigh asked.

"I'm telling you, my brother paid for 'the works' for you and that includes a massage, a facial, a manicure and a pedicure," Gloria replied.

"Damn, he's spoiling me."

"I kinda think he enjoys doing it," Gloria said, smiling as the masseuse came out. "Looks like you're up. I think we'll all be at the pedicure bowls at the same time, so I'll see you then."

"Okay."

Tinsleigh: You're spoiling me.
Thorne: Enjoying yourself sweetheart?
Tinsleigh: Absolutely. I can't thank you enough.
Thorne: You just did. See you when you get back. Remember, casual tonight.

She still couldn't believe they were having the rehearsal dinner at a barbeque place, where jeans and nice shirts were the dress code. Then again, her first marriage had been at the country club and the ostentatiousness of it still blew her mind.

"Are you having fun?" Sienna asked as they moved to the pedicure room.

"Oh goodness, yes, I feel so spoiled right now and I'm not even the one getting married!"

"You're good for him."

"*He's* good for me."

"I think you both complement each other very well," Mary replied, coming up and picking a chair. "Man, I love these chairs!"

The women all laughed as they got settled, the staff bringing them mimosas as they began pampering their feet. She sat back and let the chair massage her while the technician soaked and clipped and filed. *Damn, that feels good.* Working out again, she had noticed callouses forming, but wasn't too worried. Hearing her name, she turned and looked at Gloria. "Hmm?"

"Thorne said to sign you two up for the Gobble Jog so I guess that means y'all will be back for Thanksgiving?"

"I guess so."

"You don't see your family?"

Shit, how to explain this one? "Well, my mom and I don't exactly see eye-to-eye since my divorce. I get along with my dad, but we usually see each other outside of family events. I've got sisters, but they're like my mom and follow her lead. Since I've taken charge of my life again, I'm trying to limit how much time I spend around those who are toxic to my mental health."

The older two women nodded before Mary said, "Y'know, when Thorne's dad and I first divorced, we had a hard time. Then, he found Sienna and I found Dave and the four of us realized that we had to be there for the kids involved. Once Tom and I realized we were better off as friends who had children, we were able to move beyond all the bullshit from before. In fact, Sienna is one of my closest friends now."

"I noticed that and have to say, I'm impressed. That's not what usually happens," Tinsleigh said.

"No, it's not, but we realized that just because we couldn't stay married didn't mean we had to be awful to one another and cause our kids to have to choose. Of course, the current situation with Roger and Thorne has put a wrinkle in it, but that's something Roger has to overcome, so we're keeping out of it. It's why we had them at our house instead of Sienna and Tom's."

"Yeah, that worked out so well," Tinsleigh said, chuckling a bit at the reminder.

"I honestly think that she wanted to stir up shit," Gloria replied. "She knew Thorne was seeing someone and her ego couldn't handle that fact. But Tinsleigh? You've got nothing to worry about where she's concerned. I've never seen him act like he does with you. Ever."

"He's nothing like what I'm used to either."

"What do you mean?" Gloria asked. So, she explained how she had grown up and how her relationship with Denny had been, and what his betrayal had caused her to do.

"Have you seen him since you started working out?"

"No, we don't exactly run in those circles any longer. I've heard he and his wife have two kids now and if that's what makes them happy, then I'm happy for them. But now that I'm with Thorne? I realize how much I was missing."

"Sweetheart, you look fantastic," he said as she came out of the bathroom, dressed except for her socks and boots.

She looked at him and spun, saying, "It's not too much?"

"Uh, not at all," he replied, taking in the fitted jeans and off-shoulder top that was tucked into her jeans, showing off her hourglass figure to perfection. "And that color on your toes?"

Her laughter rang out as she looked down at the bubblegum pink on her toenails. "You like it?"

"It's very...sassy," he replied, pulling her close and kissing her.

"Uh-uh, mister, no messing with the hair," she stated when his hands went to curl around her neck. "I don't want to look like I've got sex hair."

"I'd like to give you sex hair, but we've got to head out," he murmured, giving her a quick kiss.

"This place is wild!" she exclaimed, coming off the dance floor, her hand in Thorne's.

"They picked a good one, that's for sure."

Dinner had gone off without a hitch and they were now enjoying a few drinks and dancing before the big day. He loved feeling her in his arms and how she seemed to be enjoying herself. Sitting down, he pulled her onto his lap and nuzzled her neck. "Want something else to drink?" he asked.

"Water. I need water."

"Then that's what we'll get."

Hours spent dancing and enjoying the other people who were in the wedding party had her realizing just how much her life had changed since meeting Thorne. Turning to him, she said, "Thank you."

"For what, sweetheart?"

"You've opened a whole new world to me."

"You have for me as well, Tinsleigh," he murmured. "You ready to go?"

"Yeah."

He stood and took her hand before looking at the rest of the table. "We're heading out. See y'all in the morning or later at the church."

"Good night Thorne, night Tinsleigh!" Gloria called out.

"Don't stay out too late, bride-to-be, or you'll be bridezilla," Thorne stated, leaning over and kissing her on the head.

"Bridezille, schmidezilla," she replied, laughing. "We're not staying much longer."

Back at the house, she said, "I'm going to grab a quick shower, I feel all sweaty from dancing."

"Let me grab us something to drink and I'll meet you there."

Desire shone in her eyes as she looked at him before she nodded. "Look forward to it."

She was already in the shower soaping down when he stepped in behind her. Feeling his hands running up and down her body soon had her moaning and she turned in his arms. "What did you do?" he asked, his hand having reached the apex of her thighs.

"Um, just a little waxing, nothing much. I couldn't go all the way with it," she replied, a blush covering her face.

"Honey, it feels swollen."

"Well, it hurts a bit."

"Let's get cleaned up and I'll look at it."

He quickly washed them both and got them out and dried and she soon found herself laying on the bed with her legs spread. Mortified, she covered her face as he looked where she had been waxed. It hurt like a mother when it was done but she had noticed it felt swollen and now, seeing the concerned look on his face, she was worried. "Honey, get some clothes on, I think I'm taking you to the urgent care, you've had some sort of reaction."

"Are you freaking kidding me?" she asked.

"No, you're black and blue, swollen and it's hot to the touch, and I don't mean horny hot, either."

"Fuck."

She got up, refusing to look at him as she found loose yoga pants and panties and slipped them on before grabbing a bra and oversized t-shirt. "Tinsleigh, look at me."

Looking at him, she expected to see disgust or revulsion but instead, all she saw was love and concern. "I'm sorry, baby, that this happened to you. Let's go see what we need to do to make you better, okay? And for the record, I don't give a shit if you wax or not and if you want help trimming, I'm your man."

Two hours later, he carried her back into the house. The on-call doctor who was thankfully a female OB/GYN had said it was a rare allergic reaction and pumped her full of IV medication before prescribing cold compresses and a topical cream. And advising against sex until she was healed. The medicines had knocked her out, thankfully, keeping her from experiencing the painful debriding the doctor had done in an effort to help the situation. He had texted his stepmom who had run out and grabbed some pads for her to wear to help as well. Now, as he carried her upstairs, she mumbled, "I'm sorry."

"Why?" he asked, reaching the bed and gently laying her down.

"For all of this," she replied, her hand waving down her body. He carefully removed her shoes and socks before sliding her yoga pants down.

"C'mon, let's get you undressed and comfortable. I've got some more stuff to give you as well."

Sitting up, she pulled her shirt and bra off and took the nightshirt he offered, slipping it over her head.

"I'll be right back," he said as he kissed her.

He ran back downstairs and grabbed an ice pack and some water, grateful that Sienna had put the other items upstairs already. Back in the bedroom, he said, "Spread 'em, baby," then laughed at the look on her face.

Opening the tube of topical ointment, he carefully covered the affected area, then gave her a pair of panties and the bag of pads. "Go put this on, baby, and come back and we'll ice you for a bit, okay?"

Mortified, she nodded before going into the bathroom to take care of things. *Jeez, Tinsleigh, only you!*

"Tinsleigh? You okay?" he called out when she had been in the bathroom longer than he expected.

"Um, yeah. Just...embarrassed."

"Sweetheart, someday, God willing, you'll be giving birth to our children. Think I can handle this. Now c'mon, let's get this medicine in you so you can get some pain relief."

Once she had taken the medicine, he placed the compress between her legs and set his timer. "You go to sleep, I'll remove it when the timer goes off," he said. "Love you, Tinsleigh."

"I love you, too, Thorne."

Chapter Twelve

"Since you're hurting, we're not working out today," Thorne said the next morning when she woke up.

"You look tired," she replied, cupping his jaw with her hand. And he did, he had circles under his eyes and looked worried.

"You didn't sleep well, sweetheart."

"Oh no, I'm so sorry."

"No, no, it's okay. I will never have a problem taking care of you, Tinsleigh. Ever."

"What...what happened?"

"Well, you started running a fever, so I got Sienna up and between the two of us, we got you in an Epsom salts bath, then I got more lotion on you and got you redressed while she grabbed another compress. We got some anti-inflammatories in you, and your fever broke an hour ago."

"Damn it, Thorne, why didn't I wake up?" Well, that explained the dreams she was having.

"I think whatever they gave you at urgent care knocked you out. Well, that and the pain meds. So, we're going to hang out in here until we have to get ready for the wedding. Sleep, rest, talk. Whatever."

"Just no sex."

"No sex."

"Well, damn."

He started laughing at the petulant look on her face. "Honey, we've got the rest of our lives. I'm sure we can survive a few days."

"Well, if this had to happen, I'm glad it was to me and not your sister. That would suck for a wedding night."

"This is very true. C'mon, let's go down and grab some breakfast then come back up and chill," he said. When she went to get dressed, he shook his head no and grabbed a robe he had in the closet. "You need loose clothing."

"How am I wearing my dress and stuff tonight then?"

"Is it a longer dress?"

"Um, yeah."

"Okay, then you wear your panties and stuff and I'll see if Mom or Sienna can get you some of those stockings that go part of the way up. I think those will be too tight with what's going on and I don't want you miserable."

"Fine."

He wisely said nothing, knowing that one word had a wealth of meaning. Leading her downstairs, they went into the kitchen where Sienna and his dad were sitting and eating. "How are you feeling, sweetie?" Sienna asked.

"Better, I think. Thanks for helping him take care of me."

"Any time."

"I'm just glad it was me and not Gloria," Tinsleigh said, adding some fruit to her plate.

Both men started laughing at her comment and she blushed before muttering, "I didn't mean to say that out loud."

True to Thorne's word, they spent the day lazing around, with him making her take another Epsom salt bath to help with the swelling. "How is it looking?" she asked when she was out of the tub and standing there.

"It already looks better," he replied, gently drying the affected area. "Never again, Tinsleigh, you hear me? I'd rather you be healthy than put yourself through this because you think it's something I want."

"Aye aye, Captain," she said.

"Not kidding, Tinsleigh," he stated, lightly smacking her ass. "I've never been into spanking, but if you do that again, I'll have to reconsider my position."

She raised her eyebrows at him. "Oh really?"

"Yes, really. Now, let's get ready so my sister doesn't yell at us for being late."

"I now pronounce you man and wife," the minister intoned. "You may kiss your bride."

"What a beautiful wedding," Tinsleigh whispered.

"*You're* beautiful," he whispered back, taking in her outfit. Paige had been right – she did look like the sugarplum fairy. *And she's just as sweet too. Dammit, gotta stop thinking along those lines, old man, she can't handle that right now.*

"Thank you," she murmured as they stood and watched the wedding party pass back down the aisle.

He finally led her out and to his truck so they could head to the reception. Noticing he was quiet, she reached over and asked, "You okay?"

"Just thinking, sweetheart."

"About what?"

"Well, and keep in mind it's a general question, but did you ever see yourself getting married again?"

"Hypothetically?"

"Whichever way works."

"Yeah, possibly. Why?"

"Did you picture fancy or simple?"

"Honestly?"

"Always want honest, Tinsleigh."

"No to fancy. Hell, a backyard wedding with friends and family would be fine. Going to the courthouse would work. I had the whole frou-frou country club wedding and it obviously made no difference. Granted, it was what my *mother* wanted and she was the one footing the bill so she made all the decisions, but I hated it. Felt like a three-ring circus. What about you?"

"At the end of the day, as long as I can call her wife and she can call me husband, I don't really care either way, but I like the idea of a small, intimate wedding best."

She smiled at him. They had so much in common and dating him, she had found more and more pieces of herself. "Love you, you know that?"

"Not as much as I love you, pretty girl."

"Debatable."

They pulled into the reception venue and he helped her down. "Do you need any meds before we go in?"

"I should be okay."

"Well, I've got them with me just in case."

"I'll keep that in mind."

"You look beautiful, Gloria," she told the younger woman when they finally reached her in the receiving line.

"So do you," Gloria replied. "How are you feeling?"

"Better. I'm just glad it didn't happen to you!" Tinsleigh said, chuckling a little.

"Yeah, me too. That would have put a crimp in the old honeymoon."

"Right?"

"I'm gonna let you go so you guys can get through this and enjoy yourselves," Tinsleigh finally said.

Taking her hand, he led her to their table, glad to see they were nowhere near Roger and Marisa. "Do you think you'll ever forgive him?" Tinsleigh asked, seeing where he was looking.

"I did the day I met you. Just took me a bit to catch up to what my heart was telling me."

"Then maybe you need to tell him. He looks miserable."

He waited until he saw Roger over at the bar before approaching. "Hey."

Roger turned and looked at him, shock apparent on his face. "Uh, hey."

"Listen, I'm not happy with what happened but the bottom line is, it all led me to Tinsleigh. You're my brother and that's never going to change and while I don't anticipate family gatherings and shit, I wanted to let you know that I've forgiven you your part in the whole mess."

"I...I don't know what to say," Roger finally stammered.

"Not much to say, Roger. It was a fucked-up mess, but I'm tired of feeling like the parents have to watch who they invite to what house. Just...keep her away from me and Tinsleigh, please."

"I...I can do that. I...I think she's cheating on me," Roger confided, his tone miserable.

"Well, if she is, then cut her loose. You deserve better. You've *always* deserved better."

"You...you may be right."

"I know I am. Take care of yourself."

"You too, Thorne. And...thanks."

"You're a good man, Thorne Baker," she murmured later that night when they were curled up in bed. He had once again taken care of things for her despite her protests, then proceeded to drive her crazy making out. When she had protested, he grinned and told her that there would be other times when they couldn't go further but there was nothing wrong with anticipation.

"Not really, Tinsleigh. Just one who is content in his own skin and happy with how things have turned out."

"We leaving tomorrow?"

"Yeah, I have to get next week's workouts put together. Jonathan has been doing okay, but he needs that motivation. Although, I think he and Paige have been working out together while we've been gone."

"He's your new guy, isn't he?"

"Yes. He's finally 'getting it' and seeing some progress. I'm going to see if he wants to do a triathlon with y'all."

"The more the merrier, right?"

"Yeah, sweetheart. Now, let's get some sleep."

Chapter Thirteen

The past few weeks since they had returned from Gloria's wedding had flown by and she was in awe at how hard they were all working at the gym. Even the back-and-forth that Paige and Jonathan seemed to be doing was fun to watch, especially this morning. "You gonna let me beat you?" Paige asked as they completed a set of twenty laps.

"Hey now, I *let* you win," Jonathan said once he stood up.

"Keep telling yourself that, stud," Paige replied, grabbing her towel.

"Ah, your nicknames are getting closer to the truth," he stated, grinning.

"You two done? Tinsleigh and I need to head out," Thorne asked as he handed Tinsleigh her towel. "And for the record, at the pace you were going, Jonathan, she *still* would have beaten you."

With that, Thorne led her out of the pool area, Paige's laughter following them.

"Meet you in about thirty minutes so we can take off?" he asked.

"Sounds good. You know I'm nervous about tomorrow."

"Which is why we're heading down today, so I can work that nervousness out of you."

"I see."

"Now, I know I'll probably get ahead of you but keep running *your* race, okay?" he asked the next morning as they lined up at the start line of the Gobble Jog.

"Okay."

"And remember to breathe and keep a steady pace," he reminded her.

"I will."

"One of these days, we'll finish a race together," he said, leaning down to give her a kiss.

"Yeah, right. With your long legs? Not likely, but it's a sweet thought."

He was about to say something when the race official approached the starting line and said, "Runners, take your mark...get set...go!" before shooting off his air gun.

She soon found herself in the middle of the pack and grinned, seeing Thorne way ahead of her. *He looks good coming and going, that's for sure!*

Coming up on the four-kilometer mark, she smiled, knowing her time was good. There were no women ahead of her and the closest people were not close enough to make a difference.

He stood at the finish line, an extra towel and bottle of water in his hand waiting to see her come down the hill. *C'mon, baby, you can do it!* Seeing her pink fluorescent shirt coming over the hill, he cupped his hands around his mouth and yelled, "Sprint it out, Tinsleigh!"

Hearing his voice over all the noise, she found herself kicking in and speeding up until she crossed the finish line and ran over into his arms, a hot, sweaty mess.

"You did it, sweetheart! I'm so proud of you!" he exclaimed, pulling her close and kissing her.

"That was...that was fantastic!" she replied, taking the bottle of water and pouring it over her head.

"C'mon, let's get you cooled down," he stated, taking her hand and walking over to the small track that was off to the side for the runners to cool down. "They'll announce the winners shortly, then we can go back to Dad and Sienna's and eat."

"I'm starving!"

Chapter Fourteen

"Tinsleigh, will you marry me?" he asked.

Tears trembled on her eyelashes as she looked down at the man who had taken a knee during a New Year's Eve party. "Yes!" she replied.

He slipped the ring his father had given him on her finger and stood, pulling her into him to kiss her. "I love you so much," he whispered.

"I love you more," she replied.

"HAPPY NEW YEAR!" the crowd around them yelled out.

"Congrats, you two!" Paige said, coming up next to the couple, Jonathan's arm around her. "Tiny, let's run to the restroom."

"Sounds good. Wait for me here, handsome?" she asked, looking up at Thorne.

"Always."

"I've been waiting on him to ask you forever!" Paige stated as they waited in line.

"We've only been dating a few months, silly."

"Yeah, but I knew the first time I saw him around you that he was 'the one' and no one can convince me otherwise."

"Whatever. So, what's going on with you and Jonathan?"

"Ah, lots, actually," Paige replied, a blush staining her cheeks.

"Do tell."

"Hmm, here isn't the best place," Paige said, looking at the line of women around them.

"Fine, but you better spill at your earliest opportunity."

"I plan on it!"

They finally got through the line and were headed back to their table and some delicious drinks when she heard a male voice say, "Tinsleigh?"

Turning, she saw Denny and his wife. *Hmm, looks like he didn't exactly upgrade! Wait, that was nasty. Eh, who gives a flying fuck?* "Hello, Denny."

"You...you look fantastic," he stammered. Glancing at his wife and then back at her, she saw how he was comparing them and it pissed her off. Regardless of whether or not he had cheated on her with his now-wife, no one deserved to be made to feel like they were less than.

"Thank you. And I hear congratulations are in order," she said, looking at his wife. *At least she had the courtesy to blush.*

"Um, thanks."

"Tinsleigh?" Thorne asked, having come up behind her. He wrapped his arms around her waist and intertwined their hands so her engagement ring showed.

Leaning back, she murmured, "That's Denny and his wife."

He reached his hand out and said, "Thorne Baker, and you are?"

"Denny Abercrombie, Tinsleigh's first husband."

She felt him tense up at Denny's words before he replied, "I want to say thank you, then, for walking away because I'm going to be her *last* husband."

Denny's face blanched as he took in the tall, muscular man standing behind his ex-wife. *Why couldn't she have looked like that when we were together? I wouldn't have strayed.*

Jonathan, who had come up by Thorne, took both women at his nod and walked them back to their table. "Aw, c'mon now, it was just getting good!" Paige exclaimed.

Thorne, waiting until the women were out of earshot, including Denny's wife who had moved away, leaned in and said, "Yeah, you would have."

"What are you talking about?" Denny asked.

"I saw it in your eyes, thinking that if she had looked like that, you wouldn't have strayed. I'm telling you that you would have, you dumbass."

"You can't know that," Denny stammered.

"I may not know *you,* but I know your *type,* and no one is ever good enough. In fact, I'd hazard a guess that you're already looking around on your wife. Not that it matters or is any of your business at all, but Tinsleigh has *always* been perfect just the way she is. The fact that she wants to be healthy for herself is fantastic, but I honestly don't care if she ever loses another pound." With that, he walked away, content that he had finally had his say.

"You okay?" he asked her as he returned to their table.

"Why shouldn't I be?"

"Well, I know it had to be a shock running into them here after all this time."

"A little bit, yes, but I knew it was bound to happen."

"You ready to head home and celebrate our engagement?" he asked, whispering in her ear so their friends wouldn't hear.

"What are we waiting for?"

As they lay there just before dawn, content and sated, he said, "I may have told Denny off."

Looking up at him, she said, "How?"

"I could tell by how he was looking between his wife and you that he was thinking if you had looked like you do now that he wouldn't have strayed. I called him out on that because he's the type who would have regardless. I hate you went through all that you did, sweetheart, but it brought you to me and for that, I'll never have any regrets."

"C'mere, handsome," she whispered, pulling his head down so she could kiss him. "I'm ready for round three."

Chapter Fifteen

They arrived at the race site early so he could help her get set up. Her jitters were so bad her knees were bouncing as he parked the car. "It's going to be fine, Tinsleigh. Paige, Jonathan and I are all doing this so you're not alone per se," he said, getting out of the car and helping her out. "Now, grab the duffel bags while I get the bikes. We'll get checked in then set up, okay?"

She knew she was going to puke but nodded. "You're not going to puke," he said.

"How do you know what I'm thinking?" she asked as she grabbed the bags from the back of his truck.

"I saw the look on your face. Now, c'mon, we can check-in over here," he said, pointing to his left.

They got checked in and then headed over to the transition area. He helped her get her towel set up, reminding her of the order of the race. Snapping the water bottles on their bikes, he leaned down to kiss her. "It's going to be just fine. Go ahead and get your swim cap on. Because of the size of the race, they'll have swimmers start in ten-minute intervals. I'm in the first heat and you're in the second with Paige and Jonathan."

She took her swim cap out of her bag and pulled it over her head. Struggling to tuck in the stray hairs, she felt his hands on her shoulders to turn her. "Let me help," he murmured, carefully taking the wispy tendrils and making sure they were under the cap. "Now, put your goggles on and get them set so when it's your turn, you can pull them down, okay?"

Nodding, she grinned when she saw Paige and Jonathan walking up. "You two ready?" she asked.

"As ready as we'll ever be," Paige replied, finding a place on the racks and getting her bike set up, before opening her duffel bag and pulling out her towel.

"You know I'm going to beat you and you're going to lose our bet," Jonathan said, grinning at Paige.

"What bet?" Tinsleigh asked.

"Ah…nothing," Paige replied, a blush covering her face.

"Tinsleigh? Let's stretch," Thorne said.

"Remember that skater in that movie I like?" she asked Thorne as they waited for the swim portion to begin.

"The hockey player?"

"Yeah, that's the one. I feel like he did the first time he went out and skated."

He burst into laughter before pulling her close. "God, I love you."

"I love you, too. Why are you laughing?"

"Honey, you've been a competitive swimmer before. This should be a piece of cake."

"Um, yeah, but never on this scale."

"You'll be fine."

His heat was called and he kissed her quickly, saying, "I'll see you at the finish line."

"Good luck."

"Swimmers take your mark…get set…go!" the official yelled, his air gun going off. She hit the water and quickly found her stride. The length of the pool was such that it would be twenty laps before she could get out and go onto the bike portion of the race.

Left, right, left…breathe. Left, right, left…breathe.

Her thoughts wandered to Thorne and how he was doing as she powered up and down the lanes, her strokes sure and strong. She knew that no matter what, they would be celebrating, and she grinned thinking of the surprise she had for him for Valentine's Day.

Swim cap and goggles off, shorts and shoes on, buckle the helmet, grab the bike and GO, Tinsleigh she chanted to herself. She knew the transition times counted as well and she and Thorne had practiced as best as they could, so she was able to transition quickly and efficiently. Reaching the starting line, she got on her bike and heard the official tell her to go.

As she pedaled, she worked one of the water bottles out of the holder and drank heavily, Thorne's words ringing in her ears.

Don't forget to hydrate. Eat a protein bar. You're going to need it.

I wonder how the others are doing? She had passed Paige during the swimming and knew that she was somewhere between Thorne and Jonathan. The other man had worked his ass off training, but she felt she would be able to pass him at some point if she kept focused. As for Thorne, she had no chance in hell of catching him because he was in the elite group time-wise.

Seeing the marker letting her know she had one kilometer left, she shifted gears and increased her speed while eating a protein bar. Thorne had told her that after the other two portions, the run would likely be difficult and she wanted to be ready. She came through the bike finish line and quickly got off and hurried over to the transition center, re-racking her bike and removing her helmet while she changed to her running shoes.

I wonder how she's doing? As he crossed the finish line and moved off to the side to cool off, accepting a towel and a bottle of water, his thoughts were on her. He knew from their practices that she was usually about fifteen minutes behind him, so he hit his stopwatch and started walking in order to cool down. He'd do his stretching when she was finished.

"C'mon, Tinsleigh, pick it up!" she heard Jonathan yell as she passed him. Nodding to show she heard him, she increased her speed, pumping her arms and breathing deeply. *Well, as deeply as possible considering she was on the last leg of a sprint triathlon.*

Spotting the finish line ahead, she started sprinting, knowing she had enough left to push it and get a good time for her first-ever triathlon.

"You did it, sweetheart!" he called out before picking her up and spinning her around. "I'm so proud of you."

"Thorne, I'm all sweaty!" she exclaimed.

"Don't care, Tins," he stated, pulling her close and kissing her. "C'mon, let's get you cooled down and then we'll stretch okay? I figure we have a good thirty minutes or better before the rest of the participants finish up."

"How do you think I did overall?" she asked as she was given a towel and a bottle of water.

"Drink, baby," he said, taking her hand and leading her to the cooling track. She could feel the mist sprinklers they had and smiled. It felt so good on her overheated skin.

"I think you did extremely well. I know you came in before Jonathan."

"Yeah, he yelled at me as I passed him," she said, a grin playing on her lips.

"Where was Paige?"

"I think she got a cramp during the bike ride because she fell off a bit. I hope she's okay."

"Yeah, we'll be talking about that because I know for a fact she and Jonathan were *not* doing what they should have these past two days."

"What do you mean?"

"They chose to drink and didn't hydrate properly which is probably why she got a cramp, and why Jonathan was lagging."

"Well, don't be too hard on them," she said.

"I think they'll be hard enough on themselves," he replied. "You cooled down enough? We need to stretch."

"Yeah, I'm good."

"First place in the twenty-five and under females, Tinsleigh Martin!" the announcer called. She walked up and received her medal, a blush covering her face. "You did well, young lady."

"Thank you. It was my first triathlon."

"Never would have known if you hadn't told me," the man replied.

"Great job, Tiny!" Paige exclaimed. "Sorry, boss-man, we fucked up."

"Yeah, you did, but you know where you went wrong so hopefully, you learned from your mistakes."

"I sure as hell did," Jonathan muttered. "I hurt like hell."

"Looks like you two need to spend the night hydrating," Thorne said. "I'm taking my woman home, we've got a date."

"Thorne?" she asked as they drove home.

"Hmm?"

"Did you make reservations somewhere?"

"Not exactly."

What does 'not exactly' mean? Opening her mouth to ask, she saw his grin and asked, "What?"

"It means I knew you wouldn't want to be out and about, so I called in a favor and our food is going to be delivered to the house. It's just you, me, and the zoo crew."

"I approve of this wholeheartedly as long as you tell me there's a shower or a bath or something in there."

"Oh, I can guarantee it," he replied as he pulled into the driveway.

Once inside the house, he let Widget out and said, "I'll be right in, okay?"

"Okay." She headed to the master bathroom and stripped down while the water was warming in the shower. Undoing her braid, she stepped inside and sighed.

She was so lost in thought as the water poured over her shoulders that she started when his hands gently gripped her hips as he stepped into the shower stall. "Sorry, sweetheart," he said, dropping a kiss on her head. "Didn't mean to startle you."

"It's okay," she replied, turning into his arms. "Are you okay if I turn the hot water down a little bit?"

"Yeah," he said, grabbing a washcloth and getting it wet before putting some of her body wash on it. "C'mere and let me take care of you."

She stood there and let him wash her, sighing as the layers of sweat were washed away. When he turned her so he could get her rinsed, she smiled. "What are you smiling about?"

"You. Me. Us. All of it," she stated, moving her hands. "I'm happy, we're good, and it was a great day."

He began massaging shampoo into her scalp, causing her to moan. "None of that now, you have to wait," he stated.

"It feels good, though."

"Yeah, but those moans make me think of other things," he said, brushing up against her.

Feeling his erection against her hip, she moaned again, saying, "Nothing wrong with other things. In fact, it's our day today and I vote we have more fun than we can imagine."

Quickly rinsing her hair, he spun her around until they were chest-to-chest and kissed her. "As much as I would love to right this second, I want us on the bed for what I have in mind."

She raised her eyebrows but stepped back, content to watch him quickly wash and rinse himself before he practically hauled her out of the shower stall. Grabbing towels, he wrapped one around his waist and then dried her off before gently blotting her hair. "C'mon, let's get this brushed out so I can tangle it again," he whispered.

He led her to their bed and sat against the headboard, patting the space between his thighs. While he brushed and dried her hair, he dropped kisses on her exposed skin, knowing that her wiggling around was as much a torment to her as it was to him. Finally done, he dropped the brush and towel on the side of the bed then turned them so they were laying face-to-face. "Never in a million years did I think I would get so lucky," he murmured, his hand caressing her face.

"I'm the lucky one," she whispered. "I've got you, I've got those crazy animals, and I've got my health back."

He grinned at her words. She had just gotten the results from her follow-up bloodwork and aside from the obvious weight loss, her doctor was ecstatic at where all her numbers were now. Even the thyroid medicine she had to take had been lowered and Dr. Day had told her she had likely added several decades to her lifespan. "Yes, you do," he replied. "Now, I need to kiss a winner."

Leaning down, he captured her lips. Soft sighs took over for words. Gentle strokes and nips gave way to a rising inferno. As he made his way down her body, he stroked her breasts until both nipples were swollen and when she moaned, he stopped and sucked first one and then the other into his mouth, nipping and laving them with his tongue until she was writhing. Once again on the move, he reached the apex of her thighs and gently spread her legs, settling himself between them. "God, I love when you do that," she moaned out.

"I'm glad because I love doing it," he replied before swiping his tongue from bottom to top, paying attention to her clit. Over and over he repeated the motion until she was arching her back and calling out his name.

Sitting back on his heels, he looked down at her, seeing the tousled hair, the hooded eyes, the light blush that covered her after her orgasm. "On your hands and knees, sweetheart," he commanded.

Oh my God, I love it when he uses that tone! Quickly complying, she looked over her shoulder to see him stroking himself from base to tip and she shivered. "Thorne," she moaned. "Please?"

He entered her in one powerful thrust and felt her shiver as he began to move. "Feels so good," she said, her breath coming out in short, harsh pants.

"You're so tight and warm," he replied, his pace increasing. In and out. Again and again. He could feel her pussy beginning to flutter and he reached around and stroked her clit, causing her to clamp down on him and force his orgasm out of him. Long breathless moments later when he no longer thought his arms were going to give out, he pulled out of her and went and grabbed a warm washcloth.

Returning to the bed, he cleaned her up and pulled her close, opening his bottle of water. "We need to be sure and hydrate."

"Especially if we're going to do that again, right?" she asked, taking the bottle from him and drinking half of it.

"*Especially* since we're going to do that again."

Epilogue

One

Many, many years in the future

She pulled into the parking lot where the triathlon was being held and parked. Blowing out a breath, she got out and unloaded her bag and then unhooked her bike. *Dammit, Thorne, I wish you were here.* She got checked in and headed to the transition area to get set up. Nearly forty years of competing in both full and sprint triathlons kept her focused, even as her heart yearned to see him.

The bike set up with the helmet within reach, she opened up her duffel bag and pulled out the towel she used to lay everything out. Winding her braid around her head, she pulled on her swim cap and tucked the errant strands of hair underneath before putting her goggles around her neck. She pulled out the filled water bottles and snapped them into place on the bike and pulled out the protein bars she would eat while biking and slipped them into the pockets on her shorts. Her biking shoes were positioned so that she could slip them on and then get into her shorts before grabbing her bike and going to the start line.

Checking it all over one more time, she was satisfied that she would be able to transition quickly from each event. "Grammy! I'm going to count for you today!" a voice called out. Turning, she saw her oldest grandson, Micah, standing there.

"Hey, sweetie, I'm glad you're here. You do such a great job when you help me!"

"Ella and Boyce are on the trail for when you bike, and Cody and Cady will be there when you run."

"Y'all got it all figured out, huh?" she asked, a smile gracing her face. She had been right all those years ago when she told Thorne they would be an active family, and the fact that her children and grandchildren were here today spoke volumes.

"We do! It's going to be a good day to race, Grammy. I wish Poppa was here."

She sighed before replying, "So do I, Micah, so do I."

"Swimmers take your mark…get set…go!" the announcer yelled, the small air gun he used going off. She hit the water and began swimming, her strokes smooth and sure. If she were within her normal sprint triathlon times, she'd be done in roughly fifteen minutes, give or take.

Left, right, left…breathe. Left, right, left…breathe. Her muscle memory taking over, she allowed herself to think about how her life had turned out for the better the day she met Thorne Baker. They had married in a small, family and friends only wedding in the backyard of her grandparents' home, two days before her twenty-sixth birthday.

A smile crossed her face as she flipped and turned again when she remembered the day she told him he was going to be a father for the first time.

"Thorne?"
"Hmm?"

"Can you come in here for a minute?"

He had walked into their master bathroom, a concerned look on his face. Seeing her standing at the double vanity, he had come to her and pulled her into his arms. "You okay, shortstuff?"

"Yeah, honey, I'm okay. I just wanted to show you something."

She had turned him around to face the vanity and could still remember the look on his face when he saw all the tests she had done. Every single one showed positive and the smile that stole over his face had been breathtaking.

Seven months later, they had welcomed their first set of twins, Sebastian and Alexis.

"Ten more, Grammy!" Micah yelled out when she got close to the wall. She nodded her head, not losing her stride, before flipping and going back down once again. *Our kids followed in our footsteps, honey.* Each of their six kids were physically active, and two of them now ran the gym with Sebastian taking over the nutritionist job. Smiling once again, she remembered one of their only fights. Well, disagreements, if you asked him.

"Thorne, there's no way I can wear a bikini! I've had six *kids!" she had exclaimed.*

"Tinsleigh, I'm telling you that you can still rock a bikini, sweetheart. Honestly? You're probably ten pounds lighter *than you've ever been before."*

Back and forth they had gone with her growing more upset until he had finally put his hands up and shouted, "Enough! What's the real reason?"

She had finally told him that the stretch marks wouldn't be hidden, and she didn't want to embarrass him. He had come over to her and taken the suit in question and gently but quickly stripped her down before putting it on her body. Turning her to the full-length mirror, he had held her head up and said, "Look, Tinsleigh. See yourself through my *eyes."*

She had looked at herself critically. Fuller breasts and slightly fuller hips with a trim waist and toned legs. The stretch marks she was so worried about were but faint shimmers on her hips. "You...you can't really see them, can you?" she had asked.

"No, sweetheart, you really can't."

Then he had turned her again and scooped her up and carried her over to their bed, where he showed her how much he loved her. Repeatedly.

"Last one, Grammy!" Micah yelled, having come up where she had started to let her know she was nearly done with the swim portion. "Your time is awesome! Kick it up!"

She already had her swim cap and goggles off by the time she hit the transition area and quickly pulled up her shorts, slipped on her biking shoes, then put her helmet on complete with the strap before grabbing her bike off the rack and heading to the start line. "You're good to go!" the race official yelled as she got on her bike and prepared to bike for a little over twelve miles.

As she pedaled and worked on drinking some water and eating a protein bar while ramping up to a steady pace, her mind wandered once again.

"It's going to be okay, sweetheart," he said before they wheeled him into surgery.

She smiled even with the tears in her eyes, knowing that what he was having done was routine. "He's going to be fine, Mom," *Cadence said, leading her back to the waiting room.* "He's strong and in good health."

"I know, sweetie, I just hate being away from him."

Her kids had all started laughing because they all knew where their father was, so was their mother. In fact, none of them had ever seen them apart from the other for longer than a day at most. "Mom, we've already got a cot coming in, so you can stay with him," *Katie said.* "We know you won't rest if you're at home, so we talked to Dad's doctor and he okayed it."

During his rehab, the student became the teacher as she had pushed him so that he would learn to walk on his new knee without a limp. He had fussed and fussed, but she told him they were an active family and that meant all of them were active, not just her and the kids.

"Halfway, Grammy!" Coda called out, standing on the side of the trail with a sparkly sign that said, 'My grandma is better than yours!' that his sister had obviously made judging by the amount of glitter she saw. She

252

waved and kept on pedaling, her mind drifting over the years when the kids were small.

They had decided to homeschool when Sebastian was diagnosed with autism. He was high-functioning, but the school had been ill-equipped to handle his needs. She smiled thinking about how Paige had stepped in, coming over and helping her teach the kids. *Damn, I miss her and Jonathan.* Their wedding had been a showcase wedding, with gorgeous flowers and delicious foods. She hated that on their twentieth wedding anniversary they had been hit and killed by a drunk driver. *At least they were together and didn't suffer* she mused as she wiped away a few tears.

And wouldn't Thorne kick your ass right now if he could see you? He had always teased her about how her mind would wander during her races. She always had good times but found it easier to focus on getting to the next section by letting her mind wander. Seeing the finish line for the bicycling portion ahead, she geared down in preparation to go back to the transition area one more time.

"Last section, Grammy!" Gracie called out as she made her way to the start line one more time. "Only five kilometers to go!"

She nodded to show that she heard her granddaughter as she took off at a steady pace, her mind on the last year. Thorne's physical had shown an abnormality and it had resulted in a round of tests that ended in open heart surgery two short months ago. *I shouldn't have participated in today's race.* Only, she knew he would have wanted her to, so she had honored her commitment even though her heart wasn't really there.

"Here, ma'am," a voice called out before she saw a bottle of water thrust her way. Grabbing it without breaking stride, she broke the seal and drank it down before pouring the rest over her head to cool off.

"Mom, we think you should do it," Alexis had said.

"But your dad has always been at my races."

"We'll all be there, Mom. I promise."

Unable to talk them out of it, she had prepared for this race like she did every other one, and despite the slight achiness she now felt in her hip, she felt like her overall time was going to be pretty good. *Not bad for an old woman* she snickered, her feet pounding the pavement in a steady, even pace.

"A little more than a kilometer, Grammy!" Pippa screamed as she ran by. Waving, she grinned. *Can't let them see I'm hurting.* She had felt the twinge when she was biking and ignored it, and then ignored it during the first three kilometers, but now? It was a stabbing, burning pain in her left hip. *Just let me make it to the finish line.*

"She's coming! She's coming!" Micah screamed, seeing her fluorescent pink bathing suit through the crowd. "Hurry!"

"She looks like she's limping a little," Cody said.

"I bet it's her hip again," Gracie replied. She had been training with her grandmother and had seen her rub the area when she thought no one was looking. "Get your signs ready!"

Ten more steps. Nine more steps. Eight more steps. Seven more steps. Six more steps. Five more steps. Four more steps. Three more steps. Two more steps. "Congratulations, contestant! We'll have the final times posted once all the racers have finished."

Nodding to show she understood, she took a proffered towel and bottle of water and headed toward where she saw her family standing – all six kids with their spouses and the beautiful grandkids she had been blessed with so far. *Dammit, Thorne, I wish you were here!*

She approached the group slower than she normally would have, her hip now throbbing in time to her heartbeat. *Gonna have to go get that checked first thing Monday.* As she got closer, the girls parted, and she saw the wheelchair. Her eyes widened when she saw him stand and with the help of a walking stick, make his way toward her. "Thorne?" she asked.

"Hey, sweetheart." He reached her and pulled her into his arms until they were forehead to forehead. When he felt her falter, he motioned for his chair and after sitting back down, he pulled her into his lap.

"But...how?" she asked, her hand stroking the face of the man she had loved for almost forty years.

"I've never missed one of your races and I wasn't about to start now," he replied, leaning in and kissing her.

"Oh, Thorne," she said, tears pouring down her face as she looked at him, seeing that behind his smile he was tired. "You shouldn't have, I would have told you how it went when I got up to the rehab facility."

"Like I said, sweetheart, wasn't going to miss it. Now, what's the matter with your leg?"

Epilogue

Two

Even further in the future

"I love you, Thorne Baker."

"I love you, Tinsleigh Baker."

"Are you sure you can be in here?"

"Wild horses couldn't drag me away."

She nodded before dozing off. She was so tired these days and she knew time was short, but she didn't want to miss a minute with him.

"Dad? Mom? We're going to head out, but we'll be back in the morning," Sebastian said, watching his dad hold his mom's hand as she lay in the bed. Time was running short, but he knew they needed to give their parents their privacy. They'd been together over sixty years and were just as devoted to one another as they had been when they were young. He wiped away a tear, not wanting them to see that it was breaking his heart that his mom wasn't going to come back from this bout with cancer. Oh, she had fought and fought hard, but age was now against her.

"We'll see you tomorrow, Sebastian."

Once all the kids, grandkids and great-grandkids left, the nurse came in and smiled at the couple. "Mr. Baker? You're welcome to crawl in with her. You can't hurt her."

He nodded and stood, leaning down to kiss her temple. "Be right back, shortstuff," he whispered before taking his bag and going into the bathroom, where he changed into lounge pants and a t-shirt. Smiling, he saw it was a very faded "Gobble Jog" t-shirt and figured she would get a kick out of it when he told her. The pain in his chest nearly brought him to his knees but he pushed. *Not yet.*

Slipping into bed next to her, he pulled her close and listened to her breathe. His mind wandered over their lives and he thanked God once again that all those years ago, her doctor had recommended him. She had brought such beauty and joy to his life and made him a better man. He heard the hitch in her breath and his heart stuttered. "I'm right here, sweetheart. We'll go together, okay?" he asked, whispering in her ear. He felt her squeeze his hand, barely, and squeezed hers in return. "One last race and this time, we cross that line together."

The nurse came into the room an hour later and realized that something had happened. The elderly couple were spooned together, his arm around her waist and their fingers intertwined. She wiped away tears as she checked first the female and then the male, before going back out and getting the other nurse so they could make the pronouncement.

"We did it, Thorne! We finally finished a race together!"

"That we did, my love, that we did."

The End

About the Author

I am a transplanted Yankee, moving from upstate New York when I was a teenager. I live with the brat-cat pack and a small muffin dog, all rescues, as I plot and plan who will get to "talk" next!

Find me on Facebook!
https://www.facebook.com/darlenetallmanauthor

<u>*Want to read my books?*</u>

"Bountiful Harvest":
http://mybook.to/BountifulHarvest

"His Firefly": <u>*http://myBook.to/HisFirefly*</u>

"His Christmas Pixie":
<u>*http://myBook.to/HisChristmasPixie*</u>

"Her Kinsman Redeemer":

<u>*http://myBook.to/HerKinsmanRedeemer*</u>

"Operation Valentine":

http://myBook.to/OperationValentine

"His Forever":
http://myBook.to/HisForever
"Forgiveness"
http://myBook.to/MFMForgiveness

Co-written with Liberty Parker:
"Braxton: Rebel Guardians MC"

https://www.amazon.com/Braxton-Rebel-Guardians-Liberty-Parker-ebook/dp/B079DN7HSB/ref=cm_cr_arp_d_product_top?ie=UTF8

Co-written with Cherry Shephard and Alex J.:
The Mischief Kitties in Bampires & Ghosts & New Friends Oh My!
https://www.amazon.com/Mischief-Kitties-Bampires-Ghosts-Friends-ebook/dp/B06XTTP63L/ref=sr_1_1?ie=UTF8&qid=1503886742&sr=8-1&keywords=the+mischief+kitties

The Mischief Kitties in The Great Glitter Caper
https://www.amazon.com/Mischief-Kitties-Great-Glitter-Caper-ebook/dp/B074VXFP6Z/ref=sr_1_2?ie=UTF8&qid=1503886742&sr=8-2&keywords=the+mischief+kitties

Made in the USA
Columbia, SC
15 August 2021